Marked By Destiny

W.J. May

Published by Dark Shadow Publishing, 2014.

Marked by Destiny

Hidden Secrets Saga
Book III
By
W. J. May

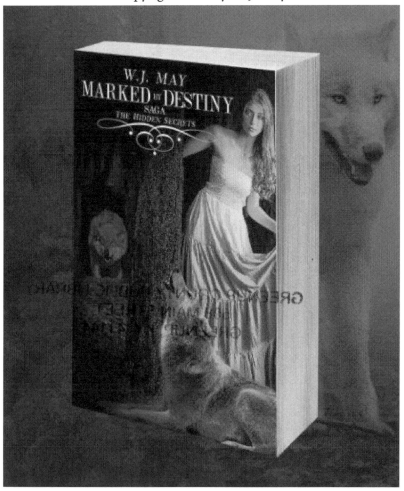

Book IV coming 2015

Hidden Secrets Saga:
Download Seventh Mark part 1 For FREE
Book Trailer:
http://www.youtube.com/watch?v=Y-_vVYC1gvo
Website: http://www.wanitamay.yolasite.com
Facebook:
www.facebook.com/pages/Author-WJ-May-FAN-PAGE/141170442608149
Cover design by: Book Cover by Design
Edits by: Chelsea Jillard
Book IV – *Compelled* - Coming 2015

Also by W.J. May

Hidden Secrets Saga
Seventh Mark - Part 1
Seventh Mark - Part 2
Marked By Destiny

The Chronicles of Kerrigan
Rae of Hope
Dark Nebula
House of Cards

The Hidden Secrets Saga
Seventh Mark (part 1 & 2)

The Senseless Series
Radium Halos
Radium Halos - Part 2

Standalone
Shadow of Doubt (Part 1 & 2)
Five Shades of Fantasy

Glow - A Young Adult Fantasy Sampler
Shadow of Doubt - Part 1
Shadow of Doubt - Part 2
Four and a Half Shades of Fantasy
Full Moon
Marked By Destiny
Dream Fighter
What Creeps in the Night

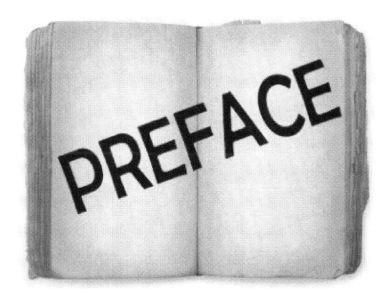

PREFACE

MY FIRST NOTE TO SELF

Well, it looks like I finally have bragging rights:

I've completed something in my life which I've done all by myself.

I finished high school!

The graduation ceremony is tomorrow afternoon – they call it "commencement" here in Port Q. As of tomorrow afternoon I will officially be done with high school. Just need to walk down the school auditorium in some silly cap and gown, pick my diploma up and it's done.

Then the next chapter of my life starts. Scratch that, a new book is beginning. I can close the door of feeling like nothing and start planning my future – with Michael.

The day after graduation Michael and I are heading across country, back to Niagara Falls. I just hope the trip won't be a total loss and I find what I'm looking for. The **real** problem is I don't really have any idea what I'm searching for – at least it won't be too hard to avoid disappointment then.

Correct that. There is one thing I know I plan to find out. Who is my mother? My father? Was what Daman told me true? Is there a way I am related to this Bentos—Ancient Journal guy? Okay, that's more than one thing. How about I simplify it...

I want to know why I ended up in the "system."

I figured the best way to keep track of the millions of questions I have is to start keeping a journal. Maybe I can find the answers to a few of them, and maybe some answers to the ones I'm too afraid to ask.

And I guess it's is time to open the Wolf Book up again. It totally annoys Michael, and Caleb even more, when I refer to Grollics as wolves but they are. They're shifters. Werewolves.

I've spent the past three months avoiding the book, but the time has come to face my future and find out what I really am. OR should I write, what I am supposed to be?! I have a terrible feeling the Wolf Book is going to tell me more than I really want to know... that's why I've avoided looking at it the past few months.

Past is past. It won't define me. I need to focus on what lies ahead, but if I want to be part of Michael's future, I need to find out who (or what) I am.

Gulp. Now comes the hard part.

Rouge

Chapter 1

I needed to know where I'd been in order to find out where I was going.

It was hard to believe I would be graduating from high school tomorrow. It felt as if I had been impatiently waiting for this moment the past four years and now I couldn't believe it was finally here. It had been my one goal for so long that I almost felt disappointed I didn't have a bigger sense of accomplishment. It has always seemed that graduation was going to be the key to my freedom.

Except everything had changed.

Not overnight. It had taken most of my senior year with a few very memorable nights and they weren't all pleasant.

I knew my goals and expectations had changed since meeting Michael. Michael was the most important thing in my life – more important than my so-called freedom. After spending my entire life in moving from foster home to foster home, I had been on countdown to turning eighteen and graduating from high school. Graduation had represented freedom from the system. I had started school a year later than most - I wasn't sure if that was because of one of my foster parents or if it was just from moving around in the system. All I remember since I was little was that my freedom would be obtained when I graduated and became of age.

Then I met Michael and my entire vision changed perspective. I spent my entire life refusing to feel hope or happiness. He had changed that. It had been one wild year. Almost a year ago I was miserable because my foster parents were dragging me across the country, a new town and a new high school. I didn't want to move from Niagara Falls to Port Coquitlam but like most of my life up to that point, it didn't matter what I wanted.

Fate seemed to have other plans.

Moving turned out to be the best thing that could have ever happened to me.

At least, that is what I knew now – someone else looking in on my life would probably disagree.

It had been a rollercoaster ride since arriving in Port Coquitlam. I met Michael's twin sister, who was also finishing her last year of high school tomorrow. Michael was already in university and this is where the rollercoaster ride starts hitting all those crazy twists and turns.

After *the* strangest incident Bonfire Night during the beginning of the school year; I learned something that would shock my world. There was a war going on that we humans knew nothing about - a century's old war between werewolves and... and... well this is where things grew even more complicated and I needed a journal to map things out. Hollywood would call it a war between werewolves and vampires, but Michael and Grace were not vampires. Sort of. They didn't need blood or have fangs. They weren't exactly dead. I think. They had died, but they had some kind of angel blood inside of them or something that prevented them from actually dying. I sighed and played with the necklace around my neck. They were, in a sense, a kind of modern day vampire.

I fell back against my bed and folded my hands behind my head. Thinking about everything made my brain itch. My boyfriend and my best friend were dangerous. They had strength and speed beyond natural human ability. Anyone in their right mind would have run without looking back. I did the opposite, I moved in with them. I moved in with an entire family – a coven – of vampires. To make things even more complicated, one of the leaders was Michael and Grace adopted father, Caleb *and* Michael was his understudy.

In fairy-tale terms, it was like dating the prince in line for the throne; except I was the peasant girl from the village – the very *human* girl. Michael loved me and had given me his *Sioghra* for my birthday in January. Everyone of their kind had a *Sioghra* pendant –created the day they died. The pendant was a small vile which held a bit of their blood – the last remains of their human blood. The *Sioghra* was to be given when they fell in love, presumable with someone similar to them because *Sioghra* was Gaelic for eternal love – once exchanged the pendants were meant to be worn forever.

Michael had given me his. Deep down I had hoped one day I would be able to give him mine. Except that would never happen. Not now, not ever. Michael didn't know yet, but I had the mark of the enemy, and one day he would hate me.

"Rouge, you ready to go shopping?" Grace came barging through the door into the pool-house-now-my-house.

I jumped off the bed grateful for the interruption. I didn't want to worry about the future. I wanted to be happy in the present. I stuffed the journal into the drawer beside the futon bed. "Almost, just need to find a pair of shoes to wear."

Grace went straight into the small closet by the door. She grabbed a cute little pair of maryjanes that would go perfect with my capris and blouse. Grace would know exactly where to look; she had filled the closet up for me.

"Thanks." I sat down on the end of the bed to put them on.

"Where's Michael?" she asked and glanced around. "He never seems to leave your side these days. I was shocked when he didn't put up a fight about shopping."

"He needed to talk to Caleb."

"And he left you alone?" The mocking shocked look on her face was too much.

"The pool house is maybe fifty feet from your place. I think I can manage on my own." I tossed a lone sock from the floor near the bed at her.

She easily reflected it and laughed. "I believe you. It's the men inside that house," she nodded in the direction of the large vintage house that Caleb and Sarah owned, "that need to be reminded." She checked her watch. "We should get going if we want to get an outfit picked out *and* be at the school for the rehearsal this afternoon."

"If we are running late we can always shop inside your closet or mine. Half my clothes still have their original tags on." I smiled because Grace loved to shop and had filled up that closet because hers was already too full. I had never had money so I was thrifty when it came to spending money.

"I'm an excellent power shopper!"

"I have no doubt, Grace." I grinned and reached for my keys hanging on the little hook near the door. I hesitated. I hadn't driven the jeep since Damon had forced me to drive it into the woods. I hadn't even gone inside it.

"I'll drive." She pressed her lips together a moment. "It's easier to find a parking space with my little Beetle."

I let my arm drop to my side. "Okay. Maybe tomorrow I'll take the Jeep out for a spin." I grabbed my purse and tried to hide the sigh of relief.

Outside, we walked around the pool toward the larger house. Instead of going up the wooded deck inside, Grace veered to the side and continued walking around the house. "Has anything changed with... you know?" she said quietly glancing up the windows by where we walked. We were nowhere near Caleb's office but she still remained cautious. Grace knew about the mark on my back. It was the same as the one Grollics had on their chest, except mine lay in the exact same location but on my back as if it had been pierced through me and ended up on the other side.

I shook my head reminded that Michael would one day abhor me. Right now though, the enemy hated me more. I had a gift (or curse, depending on how you looked at it) which allowed me to control the wolves. I could turn a Grollic into a servant if I wanted, except I had no idea how I did it. I had found this antique journal-book that seemed to explain werewolves but it wasn't written in English or any other language that anyone could read, except me. There were only a few pages that appeared to be in English to me, but not to anyone else. The werewolves didn't want me to control them. They wanted me dead.

I hadn't looked at the Wolf Book since Damon had nearly killed me back in January. Months had passed and I kept making excuses not to look at it, kind of like driving the Jeep. A part of me was terrified and the other part wanted to pretend things were normal, even if it was just for a few months. Graduation had been my mental count down. I should be excited to graduate but what would happen after, terrified me.

"Earth to Rouge." Grace waved her hand in front of my face. "You need to move your legs in order to walk." She slipped her arm around my shoulder. "I may be a speed shopping, but you need all the help you can get."

We headed around the last corner of the house to the driveway where the cars were parked Michael's mustang was gone from its usual parking spot. *Funny, he didn't tell me he had to go out. Just that he needed to see Caleb.*

Sarah, Grace' adopted mother, came out the front door as we were getting into the car. "Girls! Caleb just called and asked if you would mind stopping off at his office."

"No problem. After we're done shopping we'll go by!" Grace replied.

Sarah shook her head. "He means now, Grace."

"Fine." Grace rolled her eyes at me as we got inside the car. "Great! Kiss shopping good-bye."

Michael had obviously gone to the office to see Caleb. I had just assumed he meant the office inside the house. I waved to Sarah as Grace reversed and honked the horn at Sarah. "Do you know what he wants?" Caleb just oozed of power and authority. It made me nervous.

"Not a clue. Guess we'll find out. It had better be quick."

I had never been to the office building. I had a bad feeling this had nothing to do with Grace, but Caleb wanted to see me. My shoulder blade burned where my birthmark had turned dark. My heart raced. Could he know about the marking? Was it possible he had found out?

Chapter 2

We pulled out the driveway onto the main road spitting gravel, with Grace not even bothering to slow down; the fuzzy pink dice on her rear-view mirror swinging like crazy.

She zipped across town. I had no clue where we were going, so I stared out the window and watched the scenery whiz by.

"What's up?" She pulled around a van to pass it and quickly back into the lane. "Why're you chewing your finger nails like I'm taking you to prison instead of the office? It's no big deal."

I hid my hands under my legs to stop the nervous habit. "Sorry. Why does Caleb want to see us? Why couldn't it just wait until we got home from school or he got home from work? What does he do, by the way? I thought he basically worked from home."

Grace smiled and shot me a sympathetic glance. "He wants to see me. You're part of this family now. He's beginning to see that, so why not have you see the office building he owns?"

"He owns an entire building?" Seriously, why did this guy do?

"It's a medical building. I'm surprised Michael or I haven't mentioned it before. You know how a few years back there was this huge breakthrough in the news about no longer needing blood donors?" She didn't wait for me to response. "That was all Caleb. The man is beyond brilliant. He's the scientist who figured out how to clone plasma and blood."

I laughed. I didn't mean to, but come on, I joked about them being modern day vampires and they were the creators of synthetic blood? It was kind of ironic.

We were at Caleb's office in about ten minutes. Built completely of dark glass, the office building had a very modern look to it. I couldn't quite tell if it was five or six stories tall, as the glass architecture had a very unique design and it was hard to tell where one floor might end and a new one begin.

Grace parked in the restricted parking area, a few spots from Caleb's car. She leaned over me and reached into the glove compartment to pull out a parking tab to hang by the pink dice.

"We'll have to go through the front doors since you don't have a pass to wear inside. Next time, we can get one made up. We don't have time to do that today." She shook her head and muttered, "Let alone shop. We'll be lucky to even get to school."

I nodded, too anxious to say anything. I wanted the butterflies in my stomach to settle down before we were inside Caleb's office.

We walked around the parking area, to the front walk, and into the building. I stopped and stared. No medical building I had ever been in looked like this. Breath-taking. The main lobby had marble everywhere – on the floor, the pillars, the front desk and a gorgeous waterfall. The cascade of water was made up of a huge slab of agate that stood over eight feet tall and the pond at the bottom had koi and goldfish swimming around in it. The dark windows and incredibly high ceiling reminded me of an ancient, reverent cave. Soft music echoed softly from hidden speakers, filling the space with relaxing tones. The view almost made you not notice the cameras or security guards standing in several places strategically located throughout.

Grace led me to a room that required a security code to entire. She flashed her badge at a guard who obviously recognized her and didn't need to see it. He nodded and then looked at me with open curiosity. I wondered if he was one of them, or human like me. He looked pretty indestructible. The sunglasses didn't give me a chance to see his eyes.

We headed to the elevators. Inside, Grace hit the fourth floor, the top floor, and then put a small key into the hole above the numbers and turned it to the right. She left the key in until after the doors opened and we were about to step out. Caleb's office was obviously not open to the public –like a hidden penthouse.

The minute we stepped off the elevator it felt like we were stepping into Caleb's office inside their house. It had the same style, lighting, atmosphere, all of it. You couldn't tell if it was early evening or morning. The high ceiling lobby and glass explained why it was difficult to tell from the outside of the building how many floors there were. The windows were double layered here and his office was hidden from plain sight.

The floor circulated around the lobby. You could look down at the people and waterfall but they wouldn't see you. Facing the elevator doors was a large reception desk where a lady in her forties sat. I assumed she was in her forties until I saw the pendant around her neck, and realized she could be forty or three hundred and forty. Grace was a step or so behind me. It had taken her a bit longer to get the key out of the elevator. The reception woman's eyes narrowed and turned a lighter shade of blue at me. Then she noticed Grace and her eyes turned back to a slightly less vibrant blue color.

"Grace! How lovely to see you!" Her voice floated across the marble floor.

Odd. I'd have thought it would echo against the stone.

"Nice to see you as well Margarette. This is Michael's Rouge." It was funny to always be introduced as Michael's but it obviously was a marker that I was considered safe – or off limits. Who knew which one they meant?

"Hello, Rouge." She was very polite and smiled briefly; her face revealing nothing.

"Hello, Margarette."

"Caleb's waiting for you, Grace. He made no mention that *she* would be here as well." She nodded her head in my direction.

Grace tsked. She moved closer beside me and met Margarette's glare with one of her own, her tone turning sharp. "He knows Rouge's with me. He'll be wanting to talk to her more than me." Without saying another word Grace took my hand and walked around the glass center to the other side of the building.

The sound of her heels "click-clacking" down the corridor filled the space and our pace didn't give me a chance to ask what she meant by the comment. I thought she had said in the car that he wanted to see her, not me. My heart fluttered in frustration against my rib cage. I hated not understanding what was really going on.

She barged through his office without bothering to knock. A guard stepped forward but she held him back with a simple palm raised, warning him not to come towards us.

The office was almost as big as the cottage I lived in, and had volumes of books along the walls, along with computer terminals set up at each corner. TV monitors were set up along one wall and you could see everything going on from the floors below. Caleb sat at his desk, which was an exact replica of the desk at the house. He also had the same red leather ottoman chairs in front of the desk that he had at the house. The replication of atmospheres was almost eerie.

"Good morning ladies." Caleb stood up from his desk as we walked in. He still had the manor of a fifteenth or sixteenth century gentleman. I always felt like I was in the presence of royalty when he was in the room.

"It's nearly lunch and we're running late for school, Caleb." Grace crossed her arms over her chest. "You failed to mention to Margarette that Rouge would be coming in. She seemed slightly irritated."

"Margarette would have been annoyed if I told her Rouge was coming to see me also. Either way, I will be hearing about it after you two have gone." He let a very small smile brush his lips but it did not reach his eyes.

Grace marched into the room. "Why did you want me to come here? We were hoping to get some shopping in before we needed to be at the school for the graduation rehearsal. That's out of the question now."

Caleb ignored Grace's remark, and looked beyond her, at me. "Michael mentioned you're planning on leaving the day after graduation."

"Hi—I've..." I cleared my throat and tried again. "I am."

"You are?" Grace spun around and stared at me in surprise. "Why didn't you say anything to me?"

I stared at her, then Caleb and then back to my best friend. "I...I... Sorry." I hadn't meant to keep it from her. It wasn't a secret. Their family knew I was going eventually. Why wait? "Last night Michael and I figured it would be perfect timing." I shrugged, hating to have this conversation with Grace in front of Caleb. "I just hadn't had a chance to tell you."

Grace's face softened.

Caleb harrumphed, obviously annoyed at their female gibberish. "There are only a few days before you leave. I wanted to ask," he paused, searching for the words or maybe trying to find a way to a make his request sound polite, "I need the Grollic... I was wondering if you would let me borrow the Grollic Book to do some testing on the pages? I don't believe it's possible, but I'd like to see if we are able determine the age of the journal. Maybe test if there are any epithelial tissue we might be able to use to trace some DNA. I promise to have the book returned to you before you leave—"

"Okay."

"—As Michael also said that you plan to finally begin studying it again."

Michael using those exact words were highly unlikely. He had not pushed me in any way to pick the wolf book up. I knew Caleb had wanted me to start studying the book right after the incident in January but I hadn't been able to look at it. Just thinking about it brought bile into the back of my throat. I could feel my heart rate quicken with the anxiety pressing against my chest. I swallowed and took a deep breath, trying to calm the panic I felt whenever I thought about the book. "Caleb, do what you want with it."

"I'll be extremely careful with it and will have it back to you before you leave. I'm anxious to know if there is more you can read." He began to pace. "How you haven't been curious or tempted to read it is beyond me." He held his hand up to Grace as she opened her mouth to stop him. "No need, Grace. Michael has warned me every day to leave Rouge alone, which I have. However, if she's lost the ability to control the Grollics because of this, it will be a most definite loss." He pressed his lips and shook his head.

He did have a point. I guess I wouldn't know until I came across another werewolf. The thought didn't stop me from being annoyed at Caleb's badgering. "I'm sorry I haven't touched it in months... I just didn't have the interest to look at it. Those wolves—sorry, beasts don't deserve a minute of my time." I had no intentioned of admitting to anyone I was absolutely terrified of the book. That book might show something that was a part of me, which I didn't want to learn. Now, however, it was my idea to find out who my biological parents were so it was time to start dealing with the Wolf Book.

"That's where you're mistaken. You may have the ability to defeat them. You should have been on top of this." He sighed. "I'll ask Michael to go and get it while you are at rehearsal. He would not touch it without your permission."

I had the gut feeling Caleb had planned to take it, and Michael being Michael, had refused to get the book without asking me. He knew I was having a difficult time and refused to push me in any way.

"Whatever. Should I call him and let him know it's alright?" I was pretty sure that Michael would not bring it in unless he knew for sure that I personally said yes to Caleb.

"Very good idea."

Grace had been quiet for the past few moments now spoke. "Fine, it's all settled. Red will phone Michael on our way out. If that's all..." She looked expectantly at Caleb.

"Where's Michael?" I asked. Grace grabbed my hand to pull me back out of the office. "I thought he said he needed to see you." I spread my feet and refused to budge. "If he's here, I can just tell him in person."

Caleb looked up sharply. "He's not. You will have to call him."

Why did I have the feeling he was hiding something? I watched Caleb, trying to read his impenetrable express.

Grace finally dragged me out of the room, past Margarette and straight to the elevator. She didn't say a word until we were almost on the ground floor. "He can be such a pain sometimes! Bloody calling us to the office so he can borrow your book! Damn science labs! We could be shopping right now!"

Whoa! Freeze frame a moment. "Science labs?"

Grace waved her hand absently. "There are labs below ground at the office here. Very high tech labs – all that equipment and testing stuff. I don't get how Michael likes it. He used to be obsessed with it. It's all *so* boring! They test and experiment everything here –figuring out ways to kill Grollics, like equipment to catch them or tools to take them down, and now – but obviously not new – ways to figure out the age of mysterious journals."

"How do they test the werewolf stuff?" I was suddenly more curious to go into the basement than head to school for grad practice.

She raised a single eyebrow at me and gave me a look. "Catch a *werewolf* and use the Grollic as a guinea pig. You know, catch with newly made bullets or poisons. Bring him in here and take the poison or bullets out to see which ones were most effective."

"What do you do with the stuff once you take it out?"

"If the Grollic is not dead yet, we put them back in. And other science-y stuff like that."

I stared at her in disbelief. They used werewolves like lab rats? Or science projects... It seemed so inhumane. I couldn't imagine Michael to be a part of the dissection process. I couldn't picture it. Yet Grace had just said he used to be obsessed with it.

"Don't look so surprised, Rouge. Those mongrels do the same to us. Those idiots just don't know how to keep us alive long enough to do anything productive, to learn anything."

"I just never thought..." I didn't know how to finish the sentence.

"This is an ugly war that you have barely had a chance to scratch the surface of. You have no clue how deep this hatred goes. Caleb believes that whoever wrote that journal of yours hated Grollics. He's extremely interested in what you might learn from it, or if your gift will be of any service to us."

Shaken, I stared at Grace, oblivious to the elevator door opening and then closing again. Grace held her finger over the button with the two arrows to reopen the door but didn't press it. I was shocked – not because Caleb had plans to use me, but because Grace knew so much. Only once had we talked about how Grollics and her kind had originated. She had never talked about the war between them and the werewolves; she spent her days worrying about clothes or typical high school things, oblivious to her secret life. Or so it seemed. She hadn't missed anything; she just didn't discuss the darker side of her existence, and that realization shook me. I wasn't sure how to respond to her at first. I stood there, mouth gaping like a fish, trying to find words to use to respond. In the end, I opted for the most neutral response I could muster.

"I hardly know anything about the war, or your past, or Grollics. I plan on learning as much as I can on this trip out east."

She opened the elevator door and we left the building in silence. We reached her car and Grace unlocked the doors. Once inside, she turned back to her Tinkerbelle-self, chatting about what we had to do at graduation and the party afterwards. It was always an effort, trying to keep up with her chatter. As a supernatural she could move at the speed of light, and her mouth had no problem keeping up with that speed as well.

I pulled my phone out of my bag and pressed Michael's number.

As it continued to ring, longer than normal, I imagined him standing in a suit over some half dead Grollic, picking up his phone while aiming some kind of scientific gun right between the Grollic's eyes. My tall, blonde, tanned boyfriend all in crazy superhero costume, his bright blue eyes flashing with anger and righteousness.

"Rouge!" His masculine voice softened as he spoke my name. "Sorry it took me so long to answer. I'm at the bank and the teller wouldn't let me answer the phone." He chuckled. "She was all no-no-no and pointed to the sign below the counter that has a line across a cell phone."

The double-oh-seven image disappeared from my head. "Grace and I were just at Caleb's office."

A loud breath pushed through the phone. "Caleb make you come?"

"No." I wasn't about to get tattle on anyone. "It's all fine. Caleb can have the wolf book." Grace's eye shot over to me as she drove. "I mean the Grollic journal."

"Are you sure? If you don't feel comfortable with letting him handle it, I can tell him." His voice sounded wonderful. I could feel his concern for me – both from the phone and from the feelings emitted from his *Sioghra* pendant around my neck. "That journal belongs to you."

I didn't understand why all of them put emphasis on the journal being mine. I hadn't written the darn thing. "I don't mind. He said he'll have it back to us before we leave." I said the words and pretended to think I was indifferent but deep down I coveted the journal like a secret diary no deserved to see but me. Strange how I didn't want to admit that to anyone, even myself.

"I'll make sure of it, and also make sure nothing happens to it."

Chapter 3

"Caleb'll be careful." I knew that without a doubt. He revered the journal as some kind of Pandora's Box that would reveal all the werewolves hidden secrets. The clue to destroying them once and for all.

"As long as you're okay with it..." Michael still wanted the decision to be fully mine.

I smiled, loving him for wanting to protect me even when he didn't need to. "It's good. I won't even miss it. There's probably more dust than secrets on it now. It's still in the right lower desk drawer." I'd take the book out to hold it and touch the worn leather, only to quickly shove it back into the drawer when the urge to open it filtered through and terrified me.

"I'll go now and grab it. You going to be home?"

"Grad rehearsal first. You can come grab me if you need me." I cleared my throat when Grace pulled the car close again the curb and slammed on the breaks. "I mean, need my help."

Michael chuckled. "Do the grad thing, I'll try and stop by the school before it's over. I should be able to finish up here about the same time."

"See you later then."

"Alright." Michael's tone shifted slightly. The briskness probably meant that he was with someone else... or a Grollic had attacked him. Not like that was likely to happen in broad daylight, but it still didn't stop my mind from picturing it. I didn't know what was up with me these days.

"I'll be right back." Grace opened the car door and jumped out.

I blinked and focussed on the present. "Where are we?"

"Just a little shop I like to come to."

I checked my watch. "Grace, we don't have time."

"I only need three minutes. I had two things set aside just in case something like this was going to happen." She slammed her door and raced around the car and across the sidewalk to the little shop.

Chic Boutique.

Pretty little shop with a big front window, which Grace stood in front of holding two dresses.

The blue one she pointed at and then herself. I gave her a thumbs up from the car. She other she pointed at and then to me. She had picked out the black dress for me to wear. It was very feminine and slightly sporty at the same time.

I shook my head unsure whether or not it would suit me. The dress had no sleeves and from the front, the back looked swooping and open. I had no intention of letting the mark on my back be seen, especially by Michael. I'd managed to hide it the past few months, and didn't want to blow it now.

She tapped on the window glass again and turned it around to show me the back. It had a high back that had plenty of material to hide my back and just show off my arms. I should have known she would find the perfect dress. I knew I wouldn't need to try it on, she would also find the exact size, material and style I would need.

A moment later she came running back to the car with two shopping bags. She tossed them onto the back seat of the Volkswagen. She started the car and quickly pulled back onto the road. "Wow! That dress was made for you Red! You're going to look very sexy in it!" She let out a whistle.

I laughed off her comment, not believing a word. However, I thought that the dress did look nice. "I could have worn something I already had." There was a closed full of clothes Grace had bought me, most with their tags still one. "Thank-you for spoiling me."

She beamed, her smile spreading nearly ear to ear. "I knew it would be perfect for you! I can't wait to see what it looks like on!"

"You've outdone yourself! This moment is supposed to be monumental to *me*." I smiled, feeling her excitement. "I deserve to be dressed up a bit."

"It won't hurt for Michael to see you looking like a sexy lady either." She added with a sly grin. "Speaking of sexy and becoming a lady... have you and Michael –:"

"No!" I felt like I had shouted that as I cut her off, so I tried again in a quieter voice "Not yet. Though we are having fun working things out. We are just not in a rush to seal the deal." I felt silly talking in cryptic words but I found it more embarrassing trying to talk about sex with Michael's twin sister. There were moments where she was my best friend but moments like this reminded me that she was his twin.

"It's Michael isn't it?" She rolled her eyes. "He's so old fashioned. He was furious with me the first time he found out I been with a human. Thank goodness I never told him what had happened to the first few guys I had tried anything with!"

"Michael doesn't know that you –?"

"Goodness no! If his heart worked normal, he would have a heart attack! Don't you dare tell him now, or I will never be left on my own again!" She tried to look threatening as she said it.

I couldn't hold back the laughter. "I won't say a word! Unless of course you tell Michael something about me that you're not supposed to." Thank goodness the focus had gone back to her, not me and Michael.

"Like what?" She was suddenly interested in what I might have to hide.

"Sorry to disappoint, the only thing I haven't mentioned is..." I pointed to my shoulder blade. "And you already know that one."

"Yeah, I can't tell him that one or you'll never speak to me again." She glanced out her review mirror and added in a quiet voice. "Have you noticed any changes from it? You know, like the urge to turn into a Grollic?"

I laughed. Nobody would be watching us, and the way she asked if I was turning into a wolf seemed too comical. "Well," I said pretending to play with the hem of my shirt. "I did feel like howling at the moon the other night. Think I'm going to change?" I batted my eyelashes and tried to look innocent and worried.

Grace slapped my arm. "Not funny!" She laughed despite the fact. "If you start changing into a Grollic, Caleb's going to skin you alive. First he'll take you to the lab torture chamber and then he'll skin you."

I straightened. She may be joking but that's probably what Caleb would do. "I'm not a Grollic." I said with more fierceness than I meant. I had no idea if I could be or what I was, but I didn't want to be one. Maybe I could will it away. "Let's just drop it and head to school. We're already ten minutes late."

Grace checked her watch, suddenly probably not wanting to have this conversation anymore. "I would hate for Ms. Graid to have a nervous breakdown before tomorrow."

"True." Ms. Graid was Port Q's high school secretary, I was pretty sure she had been there when the school had originally opened in 1922.

Grace drove straight to the school and parked in her usual parking spot. I looked at the school and actually had a tiny little pain of regret about graduating. All my life, I couldn't wait for this day, and now that it was finally here, I actually felt a little sad. I had loved the architecture of the building and had enjoyed my classes.

"Grace, I'm going to miss going to high school with you. I had fun."

"Fun? You're here one year and in that year, you find out that Grollics exist, your best friend and boyfriend are living dead people, you're kidnapped by some Grollic only to find out you have a gift to control those mongrels! Yeah, definitely a year you would want to remember!"

"I should write a book and sell it."

"That my dear, could make money." Grace laughed and then looked at me slyly.

"What?" I didn't get what the look was for.

"You plan on staying with Michael forever, right?

I nodded, not quite sure where she was going with her train of thought.

She pointed to my necklace. "That's Eternal Love. Not a couple of years or fifty years. I don't want you growing old while Michael and I stay this way forever. We've got to find a way to make you one of us."

"That's not possible." I blinked and swallowed. My throat ached with the pressure of trying to hold back painful tears. I wasn't one of them, I had Grollic written all over me – all over my back.

"I'll find a way. Even if Michael won't. Just remember that okay? It's a promise between you and me – our secret."

She jumped out of the car before I could say anything and started walking towards the school. I jumped out and ran to catch up with her.

"Our secret." I confirm without saying another word.

Grace looked over and smiled as she gave me a quick hug. "Just so you know Michael's not the only one who loves you. You're like a sister to me and I want you around forever as well!" She pulled me towards the gymnasium. "I can hear Ms. Graid calling out attendance and she sounds agitated. Sounds like we aren't the only ones who are pretty excited to be graduating tomorrow!"

Inside the gym Ms. Graid stood on the stage with a microphone in her hand, trying to call out names. The physical education teacher finally blew his whistle and hollered for everyone to find a seat before he threw one at anyone still standing.

Grace saw Simon, a friend of ours, and we headed over to sit with him. No one noticed we had just arrived. Simon planned to head to Florida for university. He decided Miami was where all the girls would be going that he wanted to get to know.

With everyone finally quieting down, Ms. Graid explained how we would be accepting our diplomas, where we would need to walk and when we were to flip the tassel on our hats to the other side. She went on and on, most the kids already ignoring her and chatting amongst themselves.

"Your gowns are already hung in alphabetical order with name tags on them," Ms. Graid drone on. "You will be sitting in alphabetical order during the ceremony. No exceptions."

Grace leaned over and whispered, "I'll make sure our names are beside each other."

I raised my eyebrows at her but she just winked at me as she sat back in her chair. After another hour of practice run through we finally headed out of the school for the last time as students. Tomorrow we would be walking out as graduates, entering the real world. I already felt older than the typical eighteen-year-old. To me, this piece of paper was the final evidence of my freedom. It was hard to explain, but after spending my entire life in the foster care system and never being allowed to make my own decisions, I was finally going to be handed the piece of paper that allowed me to be considered an adult, and be left on my own.

I had already had a taste of this freedom back in January when I had been thrown out of my foster care home. My foster folks Jim and Sally were no longer going to be received government checks for my care so they had given me the honour of kicking me out. Sally had mumbled mysterious things before she took off, and I planned to find her back east when we got there. I had no idea if Jim was still here or what had happened to him. I didn't care. Thankfully, Grace' family had come to my rescue and invited me in without a second thought.

This diploma was the one last piece of paper that had kept me sane and held everything together when I wanted to fall apart.

Grace and I headed towards her yellow Beetle and parked beside it was Michael's mustang. My heart skipped. Suddenly everything felt much brighter; the sky, the grass, all the colors around me.

Michael stepped out of his car carrying a bouquet of white freesias. I knew I had a big, goofy smile on my face. I didn't care because all I thought about was my prince had come to see me. Dressed in jeans and a dark blue polo top, he looked beyond amazing. His skin was tanned like Grace and his dirty blonde hair looked lighter in the sunlight. He casually smiled in our direction but I could feel from his *Sioghra* he was very excited. The necklace gave me a glimpse of his emotions when he was near me. He was up to something or had some kind of surprise in store. I could feel it.

"Hello Red." He had taken to calling me Red since last January, when I had saved him from the Grollics. It had caught on and Grace began using it as well. I was their own little red riding hood who had saved them from the big bad wolf.

"Michael! No 'hello' for your sister?" Grace shook her head and pointed to his hands. "Your twin, your own flesh and blood?"

It took an effort to tear his gaze away from me. "Yeah, hi sis." He rolled his eyes heavenward and then winked at me as Grace's mouth opened to speak again. He cut her off before she had a chance. "Relax Grace. There's a gift for you. I didn't forget. It's on the passenger seat of your car. For the record, you've not officially graduated yet so technically, I don't have to give you anything until tomorrow."

She stuck her tongue out at him but went to the passenger side of her car to see what he had bought her. She groaned as her head popped above the car and she pulled out a new pair of bright orange fuzzy dice.

"Seriously?"

Michael shot her a beaming smile before turning back to me. He handed me the flowers. "Almost congratulations." He kissed me on top of the forehead.

"Thanks, they're beautiful."

"And smell almost as wonderful as you." He murmured.

"So Caleb let you leave the office?" I tried digging for information without appearing too obvious. "No autopsy's to preform today?" I joked.

"Funny girl." He knew me too well. "I'm curious to know what all Grace has told you. And for the record, Caleb doesn't control everything – especially me." He gently reached for the flowers and set them on the back seat of his car.

I noticed my Wolf Book lay there beside them. I stared trying to fight the burning urge to snatch it up and protect it. I hadn't seen or touched it in months and suddenly it was the only thing I wanted. I stuffed my hands deep into my pockets to appear less obvious.

Michael either didn't notice, or pretended he hadn't. "Caleb ran all the tests he needed."

I knew there had to be more to Caleb giving the book back so quickly. Fast as the supernaturals were, they couldn't rush science. "What does he want?"

"He just asked me to mention he *hoped* you might take a peek at the book before we left." Michael shook his head. There had obviously been some words between the two of them.

"He wants to know if anything's changed since January, right?"

Michael sighed and leaned against his car. "He's concerned you have been looking but can't read the book anymore and that's why you haven't said anything about it. I tried explaining the truth, but when Caleb gets something into his head, there's no stopping him."

Caleb was not one to give up easily on something. "I'll have a look."

"Please don't do him any favours."

Grace piped into the conversation, "It'll only go to his head. He'll expect it from you time and time again. Look at the book only *if and when* you feel ready!"

"Thanks, Grace." Michael threw his sister a dirty look and opened the car door for me. "She's right," he whispered, "Just don't tell her."

"I heard you!" Grace said as she jumped into her car. "See you later. Don't be back late, big day tomorrow."

He saluted her as she drove off. I waved and got into the Mustang. "So where are you taking me?" I leaned into the back and grabbed the old, worn leather journal. It felt warm in my hands and wonderfully soft against my fingertips.

Michael started the engine and pulled out of the school. "Just thought we could take a little walk before we head back home. Or I can walk and you can sit and look at the journal if you want."

"Where? The park? By the water?"

"Somewhere less busy." He drove past my old street and in a few minutes pulled into a cemetery. Not the average place a boy would take his girlfriend but it did make me smile. This was actually the first place we had met almost a year ago. I had been out running and he had just come back from... I actually had no idea what he had been doing that night.

"Want to walk or read?"

"Let's walk, and maybe stick to the paths." I said with a smile, recalling that the first time we met. "I promise not the fall over any benches."

"Or decapitate any angels?" he teased. We got out of the car. "Don't forget the Grollic book."

I flinched. Michael sounded like Caleb.

Chapter 4

I hesitated, unsure if I needed to walk first and build the courage to look at the book. I knew it was ridiculous, but that didn't change the fact: I was scared of it.

Michael came around the car and held his hand out to me, and I instantly reached for it with my own. His hand was warm to the touch and felt wonderful in mine. He didn't mention the book, just locked the car doors and pulled me toward the nearest path.

We walked for several moments without talking, just enjoying the silence together. I watched him as we walked, enjoying all his features in motion. He was tall and slim but his physique was extremely strong. It was obvious in the way he held himself as he walked or even in the casual way he would lean against the car to talk with me. His entire body was hard like the marble stones here at the cemetery, but he created a heat inside that was unbelievable.

He turned to look at me and smiled. 'What are you thinking about Rouge?"

Heat rose to my cheeks. 'Well, first I was checking you out and thinking about how handsome you are. Then I was thinking about how lucky I am to be with you. I still think you're crazy to be interested in someone like me, but I have no intention of trying to convince you to change your mind."

He laughed and pulled me closer to him. His lips brushed my forehead and teased my ear. 'You're the crazy one for choosing to be with me. I'm nothing without you. I would be empty inside if you left me." He nuzzled my neck. 'Plus you're incredibly gorgeous."

The pendant around my neck warmed against my skin, sharing his emotions. ' I think you need to have your eyes checked," I teased.

' My eyes?" He pulled back slightly, cocking an eyebrow. ' I have better than perfect vision, thank you very much."

' Maybe your brain has fogged your eyesight then."

' What in the world are you getting on about?"

I shrugged and looked past him to stare at some of the monuments. ' I'm nothing special to look at, just your typical average teenager."

' You are by no means typical *or* average." He stepped back and let his gaze wonder slowly down and then back up. ' You're tall, lean and physically fit from all the running you used to do. Your face is like an angel and those amber-green eyes are breath-taking. Plus you have this mahogany red hair that is crazy-curly one day and then straight the next. You look sexy in a pair of jogging pants and sweats!" He shook his head in disbelief and then pulled me up tight against him. ' All this," he trailed his hand up and down along the side of my body, ' is just an added bonus. It is what is in here," he pointed to my head, ' and mostly what is in here," he pointed to my heart, ' that makes me fall in love with you more and more every day. I'm the lucky one, trust me!" He kissed me softly on the lips. ' Mind you, with a taste like that, maybe I am just after your body!" He kissed me more urgently and pressed me closer to his body.

It took an effort to pull away and my body didn't like the cool air between us. I panted, letting my chest rise and fall. ' I've a feeling making out in a cemetery is not the most accepted thing. I'll feel awful if someone comes here to put flowers on a loved one's grave and they have to step around us."

Michael groaned and closed his eyes. Before they shut, their blue burned brighter than normal but by the time he opened them again, they were back to their ocean blue color. ' I didn't take you here so I could kiss and ravish you. If I wanted to do that, I would prefer a little more privacy." He grabbed my hand and started walking again.

'Why did you want to come here?" I asked.

'I like walking here. It's quiet. I figured if you wanted to look at the journal, no one here would bother you. It seemed like a good idea... this being the first place we met and with us leaving in a few days..."

'Are you thinking we won't be coming here?" My mouth suddenly went dry.

'No! Yes! I mean, we are *definitely* coming back." He sighed and shoved his hands into his jean pockets. 'I just don't... I don't know if this trip is going to change things. I want you to remember the good feelings we had here and if there are any disappointments for you on the trip, I want you to remember that there is a lot of good here."

He was worried I would be disappointed or even worse, disgusted in what I might find out about my history. Part of me wished I could do this trip on my own so he wouldn't find out the truth, but I knew I couldn't do it without him. 'I'm not expecting to find much but whatever happens, I will have you there with me. In the end, nothing really matters but that we are together."

'No matter what *we* learn; you're still going to be my Rouge, my little Red Riding Hood."

I wanted to cry. Maybe he already had a feeling I might be a Grollic or knew about the mark on my back that I was trying to hide from him. Everything was going to change after this trip. I reached for his Sioghra. Caleb would kill me and rip it from my neck before he would let Michael be with a Grollic.

Michael reached for my hand. 'How about we take one more lap around and then head back home? I'm getting pretty hungry and there's some of Sarah's casserole left in our fridge. Afterwards we can sit in the living room and have a look at the Grollic Book together. I'll help."

We both knew there was nothing in the book he"d be able to read or decipher. He meant well, and I loved him for it.

We went home and had dinner in the pool house that was now my living quarters. Michael spent most nights here. He said it was for my protection and I never argued. The conversation of intimacy or sex hadn"t come up yet. I had a feeling travelling across country without the watchful eye of Caleb might change that.

After we turned the futon into a couch and pulled the coffee table close to use as a desk.

Michael grabbed his laptop and set it on the table. ' Maybe we'll need the internet."

' Sure." I tried not to sound as half-hearted as I felt. He sounded so eager to look at the journal. ' Whoops," I said as I looked around the small room. ' I think I left it in the car."

' No probs." Michael disappeared through the front door. He was back in about five seconds.

' How"d you do that so fast?" I had just sat down on the couch with a pen and pad of paper.

' Benefits of being on the dark-side," He said with a sly smile.

' Come sit with me." I patted the couch beside.

He dropped down putting his arm around my shoulders and set the journal on my lap at the same time.

' What are the benefits of the *dark side*?" I asked and tossed the journal on the coffee table. We hadn"t spoken about what he was or what he could do in a long time. I had been thinking about it a lot lately and decided now was the perfect time to learn more, anything to prolong the need to actually open the book.

' There are benefits but like everything, there"s consequences also." He twirled a curl of my hair around his fingers.

' I"d like to know what I am in for with you." I poked him playing in the chest. ' The good and the bad."

He laughed as he reached over to stroke my cheek. ' Are you stalling? Why are you so scared to look at the journal?"

I swallowed. How did you tell the person you loved that you were wrong for them? That you didn't want to leave but knew one day you were going to have to? 'What if I am a descendant of *Bentos*?" I whispered. The truth hurt too much I couldn't hold it in. 'What if part of me is werewolf? What if I shifted and bit you? I might actually kill you! I need to find out about who, or what I am before you and I make any other decisions."

Bentos had killed Michael and Grace about a hundred and forty years ago. He had been able to control the Grollics through a gift and it was his Wolf Book that I now had in my possession.

'What did Damon tell you in the cabin?" Michael asked softly.

Since the horrific night we hadn't talked about him. My breath caught at the sound of his name and anger boiled inside of me. It took several deep breaths to calm me down but I forced myself to let it go. Damon was dead. He couldn't hurt me or Michael anymore now. 'Damon babbled on about a lot crap."

'What did he say?" Michael persisted. He shifted and leaned forward, resting his elbows on his knees.

Damon had told me that Michael had already known what I was. That Michael would never want me when I turned eighteen. I had turned eighteen and my royal wolf blood hadn't changed me. 'Damon was wrong about a lot of things."

'He said I was a destructive weapon."

Michael grinned. 'He was right on that one."

I rolled my eyes. 'Controlling and killing Grollics doesn't make me destructive. It makes me a bad person." The part that bothered me the most was that I didn't feel any remorse for the Grollics who had died that night.

'You are not a bad person. You were protecting yourself and those you love."

'Sure." I didn't want to argue with him what my conscience debated with me daily. 'Damon said I was a descendent of Bentos, and the wolves want me dead so I won't be able to carry on Bentos' legacy." Just talking about it made me angry. I was determined to find out the truth. I wanted to be with Michael and nothing would stand in my way! I had to find out about my past and my ancestry to see where I stood and what had to be done to secure my future with him.

'I don't believe for one second there is any Grollic blood in you."

Little did he know – I had wolf blood coursing through my veins.

'I'd have known that right away," he continued. 'The smell of those mongrels is disgusting and you, my dear, are freesias and honey. *That* scent runs straight through you, which is also very, very sweet. It's almost... heavenly." He inhaled and closed his eyes. 'Definitely a bit of heaven in there." He opened a single eye and grinned slyly.

'You have no idea how much I wish that were true." We had never spoken about the possibility of me being like him. You didn't find out until after you died and strangely woke up undead. Sort of like a vampire, but without the blood and bite.

Michael turned serious and leaned back against the couch, resting his feet on the coffee table. 'What I'm curious about, and Caleb and I have talked about this a number of times, I'm surprised that if the werewolves had been hunting you since your birth that they hadn't found you before Damon. You have to admit, Damon wasn't the sharpest tool in the shed. How could he figure out what no one other Grollic could?"

'That is something I hope to find out when we drive out to Niagara Falls. Maybe it has something to do with me turning eighteen? Maybe Damon got lucky and made a wild guess." I grinned. My turn to tease. 'Maybe you've got a wolf or two in one of your labs down at the office we could question? See if he knows anything?"

Michael raised his eyebrows and rubbed his chin. 'I can check."

I punched his arm. ' I"m only kidding!"

He pretended the punch hurt and leaned away, protecting his arm. ' They don"t tell us anything anyways. No matter how hard we question. They don"t talk."

I held my hands up. ' I don"t want to know." I might not feel bad for hurting the wolves, but that didn"t mean I was okay with others hurting them. *Weird.* ' Okay," I said, folding my arms in my lap. I"d had enough talk about werewolves for the moment. ' Let"s stop talking about me. It"s your turn. What about *you?*"

' Me?" He moved slightly so he could see my face.

' Besides being super-gorgeous, super-fast and super strong, what else can you do?"

He chuckled. ' You make me sound like superman." He pointed to the pendant around my neck. ' I can sense you now, even if you are a mile away; I can sense you and my *Sioghra.* You especially because I"m in love with you but others as well. All of our senses are heightened compared to humans. I can hear see, smell, and even taste better than you. "

' Really?"

' It"s like everything is better, more perfect now."

' That sounds quite nice actually. I have a hard time trying to imagine it." Another thought crossed my mind. ' What about Seth – do you remember when he came back to the house and was bleeding so bad?"

' Yeah, the wolves had given him a pretty good beating and he had lost a lot of blood."

' Could he have bled to death?"

' He would"ve died from the Grollic"s poison. It"s complicated to explain, but our strength comes from our blood. What powers, abilities or strengths we have, we lose from their poison. Seth fought against the poison and I think losing Tatiana made him fight harder. That fear of losing control and strength is what makes us fight to the end."

'Fight or flight drives you as well. Human nature."

'We crave power and strength – that is our nature. The more we have, the more we want. Some of us can control it better than others." He glanced through the window at the house on the other side of the pool.

'That"s the difference between you and Caleb, isn"t it?" I asked quietly.

'Sometimes yes; but Caleb is so strong in different ways that I"ll never be. He"s probably the strongest one on the 'good-side" and he never is tempted to go to the dark-side."

Say what? 'Now I"m confused – there"s a good and dark side?

'There are those of us out there that don"t agree to the laws of the Higher Coven. Or they don"t know about the coven – when they died, nobody was there to help them and they were left to fend for themselves. They don"t know what is expected from them and the need for power drives them crazy. There is also a Coven known as the Lower Coven. They make werewolves look tame."

I felt my mouth fall open. I assumed everyone born with some kind of angel blood was like Michael"s family.

'One moment you"re human and dying, the next you"re suddenly invincible. It"s hard not to take advantage of that. We"re all greedy to some extent. That"s human nature. Some of us just prefer the feeling of giving over the need to take."

'What"s it like to die and then all of a sudden be alive again? What happens exactly?"

Michael rubbed his chin with his hand. I could sense he wasn"t sure if he wanted to answer those questions. 'You die Rouge –your heart stops and it kills you. There is nothing pretty, nothing serene about it. Then, after a little while, your blood begins to flow again but it is different. There is no oxygen inside of it. We won"t breathe because we need air. It"s too hard to explain."

'Can you bleed to death then?"

He pressed his lips together before speaking. 'Caleb's company clones blood, for humans and for us. The de-oxygenated blood can be pumped through us and can sometimes save us."

'Why didn't you use it the night Seth got bit?"

'We didn't have any here."

'But if you know it might work, why wouldn't you keep loads of it on hand?"

'You can't store it like orange juice in the fridge. Caleb's company has tried experiment after experiment. One might work on a certain person and then kill the next instead of aiding. It's too volatile still."

'So it's a dead end for now." I hugged my knees and rocked slightly on the couch staring absently at the wolf book lying there closed and ignored. 'What happened with you and Grace the night you died?" I could ignore the journal a little longer.

'You already know what happened."

'I know you were both mortally wounded. Bentos broken Grace'back and you were stabbed. But what happened after?"

'Sarah found both of us in our kitchen and ordered her soldiers take us to the forest where they held camp. I died before in the house, Grace died on the way." Michael stared down at his hands.

'Then how did Sarah know you would wake up again?"

'She saw my eyes change before I died."

I couldn't have been more fascinated by this story.

'I re-woke sooner than Grace. Probably an hour or two after I died. It was absolute torture. I thought I was inside the house burning in a fire. It took ten of Sarah's men to hold me down and allow Sarah to explain what had happened to me." He closed his eyes and hung his head. 'I was angry. Grace wouldn't wake up and I was alive with all this strength and power. I did some stupid things that night."

I scooted over and crawled into his lap, wrapping my arms around his neck and kissed him tenderly on his mouth. 'It doesn't matter anymore."

He slid his arms around me and pulled me tight against him. ' I think about that night and what I did and it allows me to control the urges I have – when my anger wants to win over reason. I"m different from Caleb and the others that way, my conscience drives me and gives me more control of my power and strength." He shrugged. ' I don"t know if it"s because of that night or that I was always like that. I don"t know."

' You"ve never talked about this before, have you?"

He shook his head.

It made my heart beat stronger knowing he had the courage to share it with me. I wonder what Caleb would think if he knew Michael"s perspective on what had happened. What would Grace think? Speaking of... ' What happened to Grace?"

' Grace didn"t re-awaken for four days. I didn"t think she would, but Sarah was confident. Grace woke terrified. She didn"t understand what had happened or why her body was sensitive to. She didn"t move because she thought she was paralyzed. During that time, Sarah taught and explained to her what was going on and then took her away for a couple of days. I never asked her what happened, where she went, or what Sarah told her, and she"s never told me. All she remembers when she re-woke was that I was there and she was not alone."

' Wow." I had no other words to say... until another thought crossed my mind. ' When did you realize that you and Grace could communicate with each other?"

Michael chuckled and set be down beside him before standing up. ' Why don"t I make us some coffee? I think we"re only beginning to scratch the surface of your questions."

I jumped up, slightly wary of his cooking and coffee-making ability. My birthday being the exception, but the last time he"d made coffee it had come out thicker than syrup. I did not have the heart to tell him. ' I"ll do it. You keep talking." I slipped behind him and moved to the kitchen part of the room.

Michael settled back onto the couch, lying lengthwise as if on a psychiatric couch. 'Okay, back to the story. The first time I went off to hunt for Bentos, I couldn't think straight. I was driven by hate and anger. Sarah told me I couldn't go, so I snuck off alone with no clue what I was doing. I had no idea how to hunt or track. I was also terrified someone from town would recognize me since everyone believed Grace and I had been killed, along with my parents, by the fire in the house. So I took off running – and that is something a newbie with super-fast ability should never do."

'What happened?" I grabbed two mugs out of the cupboard and set them by the Keurig.

'I got lost. I couldn't believe how fast I could run and that I wasn't getting tired. I tested my limits and well, I got lost. Suddenly I heard Grace calling for me and I thought she was right with me. Her voice came through so clear I honestly thought she was right behind me. I must've looked like an idiot turning around to answer her and then found no one by me. She spoke again and I finally realized it was in my head. I guess she told Sarah because a short while later there were two of Sarah's scouts leading me back to the camp. Of course, Sarah was fascinated with our talent because she'd never come across it before."

Happy home-maker Sarah used to be a tough military sergeant. No wonder Caleb fell for her. 'Did she train you and then send you off to find Bentos?"

Michael shook his head. 'I did it on my own. She never stopped me or told me to let it go. Sarah let me go, even when Grace begged me to stay." He huffed and let a sharp breath out through his nose. 'I spent about five years trying to hunt the bastard down. It became my complete focus. I was close so many times but he eluded me or would send werewolves in to attack and he'd manage to escape. It was consuming me and Grace continued pleading with me to let it go. Finally one day I just realized enough was enough. I needed to move forward with my life instead of being stuck in the past."

I poured milk into the coffee and added a touch of sugar to mine. Walking back to the couch, I set them down on the table to cool. 'So you returned and you guys have been together ever since?"

'I came back to Grace, and talked things over with Sarah. We didn't stay. Grace and I went on our own for a few years but eventually came back. Sarah knew we would; she was our home. We'd settle somewhere for four to five years and then move to the next town and kept doing that so the non-aging thing didn't appear too obvious. When Sarah met Caleb, he liked the idea of settling into one town and moving when needed. He wanted to study and experiment without having to cover his tracks. It was only about fifteen years ago that he figured out how to clone human blood and plasma. It took the world by storm. His company is the only one able to produce the cloned blood – no human has been able to copy or repeat the process. It makes Caleb a very, very rich man and gives him the freedom to do as he pleases. Money can buy a lot of things – and not just material wealth. No one knows that he is the owner; he is the unseen face of Fuilteach Corp."

I had seen the Celtic looking FC symbol from the company on many things but never realized who, or what, the company was. 'So Caleb started the company? Hasn't it been around for like a hundred years or something?" I remembered seeing commercials and some centennial motto on it."

'You got it. He's the original owner. What do you think Fuilteach means?"

'It is some easy answer? Like the corporation want to the fuel to teach and learn?"

Michael smiled. 'Most people probably assume that's the explanation. However *Fuilteach* is actually Gaelic for 'bloodthirsty." Caleb's mother was Irish and he uses a lot of Gaelic terminology. His sole purpose for starting the company was to use science to figure out how our blood changed when we died, and what made us continue to live. Then he wanted to stop Grollics, and the company"s grown and grown."

Figures Caleb would use a name so obvious, yet undetected to the human eye. It also didn"t surprise me if he used the government to help fund his research. He probably justified it by selling them the cloned blood and plasma. At the end of the day, he was a business man – an excellent business man. "When we were at the building today, Grace mentioned that there are labs in the basement. Do you work down there?"

"I"m upstairs. My office is connected to Caleb"s. I have access to Caleb"s office and through the hallway. You probably didn"t notice the door as it blends into the wall. I used to work down in the labs. Caleb would like me to do more but I just do not have the commitment to the science that he does." He shrugged his shoulders like it was an argument he had daily with Caleb.

"I"m sorry you"re stuck in a job you don"t really want to do."

"Don"t get me wrong, Rouge. I love my job. I hunt down the bad guys. I am set to inherit a kingdom of a company."

The way he said it, I knew he didn"t mean the last part. He didn"t want the corporation, but he felt obligated to follow in Caleb"s footsteps. Hopefully that day would never happen. "What can"t you stand about it? There has to be parts of what you do you wish you didn"t have to."

"So basically you are asking me: What do I hate about being me?" A bitter laugh escaped his lips.

I nearly knocked my mug over as I reached for it. He had sounded like Caleb when he had spoken then. "Sorry, that came out a lot harsher than I intended."

"Be glad you are not one of us. It is hard to explain how I feel. I"m not talking about *who* I am but *what* I am. I"m here forever; not allowed to grow old, or die peacefully. I can"t have children or grandchildren." He reached for my hands and held them tight. "I would trade this entire life of eternity to be with you for the next fifty-sixty years – *that* would be enough of a lifetime for me."

I opened my mouth to speak, but Michael didn't let me.

' I have no soul; I forfeited that the night Bentos walked into my parent's home. I have to live like a nomad, I don't really have a place to call home but for a few years and to us, it's just a blink of time. I have to watch where I go, watch my back, watch what I say or how fast I move, watch this, watch that, watch and wait every minute of every day. That was why I didn't want you to get close when we first met. It still tears me up inside. I love you and want you to have every experience you are entitled to – the good and the bad." He stopped talking and turned to look out the window, torn by his feelings and his wants.

' Michael," I said quietly waiting until he finally turned to look at me. ' I've had enough of being alone, of being an outsider, to know that what you have and how you feel is more than I've had in my lifetime. I can't imagine my life without you, nor can I think for one moment of you living your life without me. I also don't believe that your soul is gone or forfeited – what happened to you wasn't by choice. Maybe there is a real reason why you are supposed to be around this long – possibly to help me or someone else." He could die, I knew because of what had happened to Tatianna. The thought burned in my throat and cut through my heart. I wouldn't ever let that happen while I was with him. ' I don't believe you're a nomad; you've had more of a home here than I have my entire life. You have given me a place to call home and I am not talking about here in this cottage I am talking about here," I pointed to his heart and leaned forward to kiss him on the lips.

' Don't try to make..." he tried to stop me leaning onto him but wasn't trying very hard.

' You may not think you're alive but trust me Michael, you are. You feel love and passion and I *know* you feel lust. I think you might need a little reminder lesson in that area."

'A lesson? You think you can teach me something?" he teased, all previous conversation forgotten as I watched his eyes turn to their familiar shade of blue.

'I might be able to teach you a thing or two. After tomorrow's graduation, you are going to be with a free girl, maybe we can work on making that girl into a lady at some point."

He chuckled at my choice of words. I lowered my lips towards his neck, and quickly cut off the laughter. It turned it into a groan as his arms came around my body.

I had no intention of working on the Wolf Book tonight and now we wouldn't be. Caleb would be disappointed but he could wait. That book was my past, my future. It was none of his business unless I choose to share it.

Michael distracted me as his hand roamed over my thin shirt squeezing my breast tenderly. My fleeting thoughts of the book were completely forgotten.

Chapter 5

I woke, and knew it had to early by the lack of light and the birds chirping outside. Without opening my eyes, I knew I was alone. I enjoyed nature's sounds before finally opening my eyes and rolling over toward Michael's side of the bed. His spot felt cool. He must have left a while ago. A note and an origami flower sat on the table beside the futon.

Gone to get an oil, lube and filter for the Jeep so it's ready for travelling tomorrow. I'll bring you Starbucks.

I checked my watch. Barley six. Michael would probably be an hour. Closing my eyes, I inhaled and rolled onto my back.

Two minutes later I kicked off the sheets, no longer tired. The Wolf Book lay on the table, shifted to the far side and nearly falling off. I might have knocked it last night, I couldn't quite remember.

I poured myself a glass of orange juice and came back to bed, grabbing the journal and tossing it onto the mattress as I sat on the duvet cross-leg. I drink and stared at the brown worn leather of the cover. "Screw it, just do it," I mutter.

I leaned over to snatch Michael's pillows, and then propped them up against mine so I could sit on the bed and be more comfortable. Butterfly wings beat against my stomach. I wiped my palms against my shirt and tried to decide whether it was nerves or excitement going on inside of me.

My fingers curled around the top right corner of the book, and I flipped it open to a random page. Why start at the beginning? It didn't matter. The flippin' thing was written in a foreign language, some kind of ancient dialect that nobody seemed to have heard of, like a secret code.

I stared up at the ceiling before finally glancing down to see where I had ended up. The page has a rough drawing of a Grollic in human and shifted form. The diagram focussed on the heart, showing how it moved from the left to the right side of the body as it shifted. A note box on the side of the drawing caught my attention. There was a flower drawn beside the words. "Weird, never noticed that before." I read it several times before finally reading it out loud slowly. I couldn't seem to grasp the whole message.

"For Grollics refusing to obey: Carry pen with a pure silver pointed tip. Grind aconite. A knife or any extremely sharp point will suffice. Cloth wet with aconitum, pen wrapped inside is perfect for travelling or in a bind. Must be careful, it is toxic to all in large doses. Stab Grollic and he will drop in pain. Prefer to stab in animal form but it will work on human too. Stab or prick near heart and Grollic will die too soon. Don't kill immediately – first determine what side they are on."

I had no idea what aconite was so I grabbed my phone and googled it. I sniggered. *Of course – it's called wolfs bane.* The little drawing by the box was an aconite flower. Pictures online showed it clearly. My head popped up as my brain processed the last sentences. "Don't kill yet? Huh? Wait. There are sides?" Wolves had sides – did Michael know that? Did Caleb?

The rest of the page looked the same to me as it did six months ago. I must have somehow missed the writing by the drawing. Or it magically appeared. With the book, there was no telling.

I began flipping through the pages, going backwards. I wanted to find the Red Riding Hood story again. My thumb caught too many pages or I flipped too fast and ended up right at the beginning, on the second and third page.

I glanced down and my breath stuck in my throat. "Nooo..." I double checked to see if a page might have slipped out while Caleb had the book. Maybe he just stuffed it back in the beginning. Except all the pages lay sewn in with the same antique thread – probably wolf hair – nothing was loose. I blinked several times to try and clear my eyes. It made no difference.

"For Pete's sake..." Words once written in some unknown language were now in English. On both pages! My heart hammered against my chest. "Impossible," I whispered. Last January I could only read the middle section of the book, or the 'heart' of it as my graduating English teacher would say.

With shaking hands, I slowly turned the page over. More English! My shoulder muscle twitched. It could have come from my hidden mark or maybe my brain unconsciously triggered it. I flipped to the back pages of the book and released a breath I didn't know I had been holding.

The foreign language was still on those pages.

I slammed the journal shut and tossed it across the bed. Dropping onto my back I shook my legs to relax my muscles as I tried to calm the hysteria building inside me. Why hadn't I looked at this sooner? For the stupid reason of wanting to feel like a high school kid for a few months? No wonder Caleb wanted me to look and Michael had grown impatient. I'd have done the same. What if there were things in the journal to stop the Weres once and for all?

Or I could be completely wrong and reading the opening chapters would turn me into a Grollic. My mouth went instantly dry. "That can't happen," I told myself unconvincingly

Maybe the middle section of the book had given me the power to keep the shifting at bay. "Like some voodoo witch spell." If werewolves existed, why not witches?

I grabbed the book and held it tight in both hands. *"Please, please... just let it be back to normal."*

I opened the book again to the first page and sighed. English. I scanned the first page and realized what it was. I had just bought one of these and decided to try and write one.

A damn journal.

My annoyance spurred a degree higher when I noticed the signature at the bottom. *Bentos*. I banged the book closed a second time, this time throwing it against the wall as hard as I could.

I stood. "Damn it! Why? Why me?!" I hollered.

A millisecond later the door swung open and Michael burst through. "Rouge! What's wrong?" Half crouched, ready to attack, his eyes darted around the room trying to access the situation.

Surprised by his sudden appearance, I jumped back, lost my footing and fell onto the bed. I lay muttering a string of obscenities while I pummelled my fists against the mattress.

"Rouge, what's wrong?" Michael rushed to my side, touching me to make sure I was alright.

I pushed his hands away and sat up feeling guilty to cause the concern etched on his face. "Check the book. You'll see the problem."

He paused before walking across the room and picked the journal off the floor. "Did Caleb do something to it? I told him if he did..."

"It's not Caleb's fault. At least I don't think so." He couldn't have changed the words, could he? "Hey," I said pointing to his hands. "Where's my latte?"

Michael rolled his eyes as he glanced quickly up from the book before returning ha bewildered gaze to me. "By the front door currently being enjoyed by the grass. I was more concerned about your safety than your latte."

"Darn." Totally my fault.

"So *what* was the screaming about?" He held the book open and came back to the futon.

"I wasn't screaming."

"Stop stalling and answer the bloody question."

The irritation in his voice annoyed me. I knew it wasn't his fault but I had to blame someone... or take my frustration out on someone. "Look at the beginning of the freakin' book!" I snarled.

His face softened. "You can't read anything can you? Nothing's changed? It's alright, Rouge. It doesn't matter."

I didn't need his sympathy. It just aggravated me more. "I wish! Look at the damn first page!" He was going to freak when he saw it was from Bentos.

He looked down and then finally at my face. Eyebrows raised, he glanced down at the book again. "What do you see, Rouge?"

Double crap. The words changed only for me. An odd thought crossed my mind: If I spoke French, would the words have converted to French? Or any other language?

I pressed my lips tight together. I should've checked the stupid thing months ago.

Michael looked up, waiting for me to answer his question.

I let out an exasperated huff. "The first part. It's in freakin' English. I can read it!" I shook my head. "The middle and now the front." I collapsed back so my head hits the pillow. "I don't know what I did."

"Why are you disappointed? This is exactly what Caleb was hoping for."

"I'm glad Caleb's so happy." I snapped and then instantly regretted the words. It wasn't Michael's fault that I could read the book. "I'm sorry. I've been avoiding the book and had really hoped nothing would change. I thought my reading the middle section was a fluke and the incident back in January maybe a one-off." It was all too real and concrete now. I was mad because I had known it all along, I just hadn't wanted to admit it. Daman had wanted me dead, how many more were lining up? I'd wasted so much time.

"What does it say?"

"I haven't read it yet." Suddenly I wasn't sure I wanted to tell him whose book it was.

"Oh." He sounded disappointed. It broke my heart.

I had to tell him. "I know *what* it is."

"Pardon?" He scratched his head.

"The first part of the book is a... journal."

"So?" He shrugged, not understanding what I was getting at.

"Written by *Bentos.*"

"So wh—*what?!*" His eyebrows furrowed together. He dropped the book like it burned him. It landed on the bed beside me with a soft thump.

It was all too much. I was graduating that day. I didn't want this kind of weight on my shoulders now. I let my head drop against my knees. The diary by Bentos confirmed what I didn't want to admit. If Bentos wrote the book and only I could read it, then Damon had told the truth. I was a direct descendent of Bentos. Michael would hate me. This book found its way into my hands by fate, or destiny, or whatever. That fateful day back in January when I spoke the ancient language and controlled the wolves was not a fluke – it was in my blood.

I'm supposed to be able to read it. My eyes filled and I bit my lip, trying to hold back the tears. I didn't want this book or this ability.

Michael kneeled beside me. He tucked a strand of hair behind my ear. "Rouge, it's going to be fine. It's a rare gift. It doesn't mean *you* are Bentos." He placed a warm hand against my shoulder.

I swallowed hard. Images of Grollics, markings, pictures from the journal swamped my vision. "What happens if reading this book changes me?" I was on the verge of tears, desperately trying to fight them back. I pushed the worry of Michael to the back of my mind, unable to handle it at the moment. "What if it turns me into a werewolf?" I whispered. Suddenly I didn't want to know anything about my past. Going to Niagara Falls seemed like the biggest mistake in the world.

"It won't. It can't. Maybe the journal part of the book will help you understand what not to do. It might teach you how Bentos was able to control the Groll—wolves."

I tried to smile. He was trying so hard to make everything be okay, even referring to the Grollics as wolves. He still didn't have a clue about the mark on my back. "I don't want to control them." I clenched my teeth tight, my jaw muscle twitching.

"It could be useful, in the right hands – your hands." He reached for mine and held them in his. "You were destined to find this book."

He was right. I could do something useful with the journal. I could destroy it so no one would be able to use it again. I just couldn't tell Michael. Another thought occurred to me. I was the last of the line – I couldn't have kids. This book and its ability would end with me.

"Wait till Caleb finds out."

I laughed. It started out as a giggle but turned into a fit of hysterics.

"What's so funny?"

I could barely get the words out, "...I think... he's going... to... want to be my... best friend!" I held my belly. It hurt from the laughter.

Michael shook his head. "You're crazy."

"You're just figuring that out now?" I threw a pillow at him, which he easily ducked away from. I leaned forward and gave him a fierce hug. It sobered me up. "I love you."

"I love you, too." He hugged me back.

We lay on the bed a moment, cuddled together. The wall clock chimed.

I untangled my arms from around him. "Let's go make Caleb's morning and tell him I can read more of the book. The freak-of-nature has a new talent."

Michael grinned, probably beyond pleased I'm acting semi-normal again. "Freak? You fit right in with this family now." He sat up. "Do you want to see what the pages say? You know, before we head over to the house?"

I shook my head. "Nope," I said with more conviction than I felt. "I want to graduate today. I want to do it with a clear head, not full of werewolf mumbo-jumbo." I don't know why I had been so scared to read it, but I had, and another day of avoiding it wouldn't change a thing.

"Tonight... or tomorrow then... whenever, I don't care right now." Michael shrugged. "I'm just happy you opened it and saw it had changed."

"Thanks." He understood my hesitation, but I didn't understand his new eagerness in my looking at the book 'finally'. "I don't know what I would do without you."

"Probably be a normal eighteen year old human girl." He smiled ruefully as he pulled me up from the bed. We headed to the front door of the pool house. I squeezed his hand, realizing that he somehow felt responsible for what happened to me – like being with him caused me to be able to control the Grollics.

We walked into the house through the back door, and into the kitchen. No one was there, so we headed straight to Caleb's office off of the living room. Michael didn't even bother to knock, he just opened the door and stepped in.

Chapter 6

Michael barged in. "Rouge looked at the book. She can read more." Straight to the point, no pleasantries.

Caleb's head shot up from the paper he sat reading. One moment he was behind his massive desk and the next he stood in front of me, before I could even realize he had moved. "What does it say?"

I hated how Caleb always made me nervous. It made it hard to focus when he was uber intense. I didn't know if it was because I feared him or if it was something else, but suffice to say, it never leant itself to great communication between the two of us. "The first part of the book's in English now."

"Same as before?" He looked at Michael for confirmation.

"Yup," I said loudly, my nervousness giving way to irritation. I hated it when he did that, like I wasn't capable of answering a simple question. "*Still* written in the ancient stuff but it's English to me. *Same* as the middle section."

"What did it say?" He repeated

"Caleb," Michael answered for me, "Rouge just realized it. We came over here to tell you. She hasn't read it."

I appreciated that Michael made it sound like I wanted Caleb to know immediately. Caleb turned to smile at me. The smile sent chills down my back, but I made an effort to smile back. It was obvious he didn't believe I hadn't read it. Either that or he couldn't fathom why in the world I wouldn't and he took me for an idiot.

He walked back around his desk. "Then have a seat and start reading it out loud. Let's all hear what it has to say."

"The book's still in the pool house."

"Go get it then."

Michael shook his head. "No."

Caleb rose his eyebrows and looked at Michael incredibly. "Excuse me?"

"Rouge graduates today. Let her do it with a clear head. We'll start the book tomorrow. There's more to read, that's all you need to know. Now leave it alone."

"What?" Caleb roared.

"Tomorrow." Michael said firmly. "I've done what you asked. Leave her alone today about it... and don't hound me." He took my hand and led me, mouth hanging open, out of the office.

I had no idea what just happened. I leaned toward him, about to whisper why he didn't just tell Caleb the first part of the book was the journal written by Bentos, but Michael put a finger to my lips and shook his head.

"Michael!" Caleb hollered. "Get back in here!"

I paused but Michael tugged my hand to keep me walking. "Let's just go."

Caleb barged out of his office. I could hear him stomping behind us and I cringed as the sound got closer. "What the hell is the matter with you?"

I felt Michael's hand tense in mine. I had a feeling being the middle of the two of them was not a good place to be.

Michael swung around, pulling me to the side as he marched inches away from Caleb. He stood half a foot shorter and Caleb looked down on him as Michael glared up. "Nothing's wrong with me.

"Do you forget whose side you are on?"

"I know exactly where I stand." Michael's hands moved emphatically as he spoke. "I've known it all along. Nothing's changed."

"Like hell it hasn't." Caleb's crossed his arms over his chest.

"What are you talking about?" I asked. It seemed like they were moments away from tearing each other apart and I was the only one in the house to stop them. Not an enviable position for me.

Caleb didn't even glance in my direction. "Michael's my understudy. He's not yours. No lapdog is going to come around and take him away from this coven."

"She's not a lapdog," Michael hissed. "You think she's the weapon you need against the Grollics. I'd watch what you say."

"Why? She's not going anywhere. The Grollics don't want her, her family didn't want her. We're the only ones she has."

I expected to feel shock at the words, an immediate stab to the heart or something. I didn't have the chance, because Michael defended me before I even realized Caleb had hurt my feelings.

"She only needs me. Push me too far, Caleb, and I'll walk away and never come back."

Caleb grabbed Michael by the throat and lift his off his feet.

"Stop it!" I screamed desperately scratching at Caleb's arm, trying to force him to release Michael. I couldn't believe this was happening. Caleb was supposed to be excited about the book. He's the one who had been pushing for me to see it. I was graduating soon and today was supposed to be a fantastic memorable day. "Let go of him!"

Caleb released his grip and took a step back. Michael charged at him the moment he touched the ground. He tackled Caleb around the waist and the two of them went flying, crashing into a table and against the wall. They rolled on the ground and bumped into the couch. Michael stood first and using both hands, picked Caleb up by his throat.

Caleb grabbed and thrashed against Michael's hands but could not break free. I watched in horror. Could Michael kill Caleb? Would he?

"Are you done?" Michael said in a quiet, demanding voice.

Caleb stopped struggling and gave a curt, almost unnoticeable, nod.

Michael let him go and turned away. The anger inside him burned his eyes a bright blue that I had never seen. I stepped back as he came closer.

Caleb straightened his clothes. "She's not worth losing your family over, Michael."

Michael ignored Caleb as he put his arm around me and led me through the kitchen to the back door.

"She's just the messenger. She'll turn on you for her pack. You'll be left with nothing. Or worse, left for dead."

We left the house and headed back to the pool house in silence. My mind was reeling. What did Caleb mean?

Michael held the door open for me. I couldn't hold it in any longer. "What's going on?"

"Nothing." His eyes had turned back to their normal shade of blue. "Caleb's a dickhead. He's just mad you wouldn't tell him what it says in the book."

What? Michael was the one who told Caleb he could wait. "Why didn't you let me tell him Bentos wrote the book? That it's his journal?"

Michael slammed the door. "You said you wanted today to be about your graduation! If you tell Caleb the book's a journal, he's going to want you to read it and tell him what it says! He wouldn't be satisfied – he never is." He threw his hands in the air.

So Michael had fought with Caleb because I said I wanted to focus on graduation today? That didn't make sense. There had to be something more. I knew it. "Will it change things if Caleb knows Bentos wrote the journal?"

Michael let out an exasperated sigh. "Tell him after the ceremony, then. It won't change anything if he knows that information later today or after we leave. Do what you want."

I nodded my head, as if it made total sense. None of it did, but Michael was obviously in no mood to talk and I had a feeling that if what was really going on would hurt me in any way, he'd protect me from it until his dying breath, which also meant it was going to be difficult to find out the truth.

A knock on our door made me jump.

Grace walked in hands full of bags, oblivious to the tension between Michael and I. "You ready for me to do your hair, Rouge?"

"Where you just at the house?" Michael asked her.

"Hello to you too, brother." Grace laughed. "I haven't been inside the house yet. I left to grab some hair products and run a few errands. Why? What's up?"

"Nothing." He grabbed his car keys off the small table by the door. "I'll get out of here and let you get ready." He brushed past her for the door and then paused a moment before turning around. He glanced at me but wouldn't look me in the eye. "Have fun. What time do I need to be back to pick Rouge up?"

Grace waved her hand as she dug through one of the bags. "Rouge and I can drive together in my car. You can go with Sarah and Caleb." She glanced up when he snorted. "Or on your own if you want?" Her last line came out more as a question than a comment.

Michael nodded. "See you there." He disappeared out the door.

Grace held up three kinds of hair irons. "You want it curly? Straight? Or both?"

If Michael wasn't going to say anything to Grace, neither would I. "What do you think?" I grabbed one of the stool chairs and set it by the counter. "Do we need anything from the bathroom?"

"Nope. I have it all here." She set several brushes, combs, hair products on the counter. "Sit and let me play dress up!"

Grace straightened my hair, applied my make-up and got my dress out, babbling the whole time. It was a blessing. It gave me time to let everything settle and regain my equilibrium. She did her hair and then ran back to the house to get dressed as I changed.

I waited impatiently for her to return. I had no intention of going inside the house to get her. I just wanted to get out of the pool house and stop thinking about the Wolf Book and all the chaos that surrounded it.

The book lay on the coffee table where Michael had put it this morning before everything had blown up uncontrollably. I checked my watch. We didn't have to be at the school for another twenty minutes. I ran the warm, worn leather binding over my hand.

What would happen if I read the first page, just to see what Bentos had written? Would it give answers to what had happened this morning?

Grace's silhouette passed by the windows as she came back up to the pool house. It would have to wait. I set the Wolf Book on top of the diary I had started writing. If I kept the two books together I could pack them later that evening to take along in the Jeep. I made a mental note to write something in my journal after graduation. I should be trying to capture my feelings while they were fresh, not later on when I would just tell the story and forget the emotions I had felt while it happened.

Chapter 7

As Grace and I drove to the high school in her little yellow Beetle for the last time, I sat quiet, staring out the window lost in thoughts of uncertainty. I tried not to think about what Caleb had said but I couldn't shake the fact that he was hiding something, and Michael was too. I felt cheated. A little voice inside told me that I was hiding things as well. We all had secrets.

Grace chattered on about what the other girls would be wearing, that she was looking forward to taking a few courses in university next fall. I nearly laughed out loud when I tuned in to what she was saying. I knew she wasn't interested in the classes, but the boys that would be on campus.

"I'm ready for a little fun," she said. "These high school boys are much too young and can't handle anything. I need to find a nice young professor and play around a little."

I turned away from the window and stared at her. I'd hit the nail on the head. I giggled and tried to keep a straight face at the same time. "Interesting concept you have there on your university education."

"You go ahead and laugh!" She shook a finger at me teasingly. "You have Michael and I've had no one since Seth left."

"Excuse me?" Seth was part of the Higher Coven, like a way younger brother to Caleb. He had helped us out last January but had also lost his partner Tatianna, in a fight with the werewolves. "You and Seth?" He was younger than Caleb, but still...

"Oops, I could have sworn I told you." She grinned at me slyly.

"You told me nothing!" Seth seemed to be quite the lady's man but there was a unique connection between him and Grace. This morning's incident forgotten, I pushed her for info. "What happened?"

"Not much."

"Liar!" I laughed.

"Okay. Maybe a bit of... lustful-limbo."

"Lustful limbo?" I laughed again. 'Seriously? Did Seth or you call it that?" Another thought crossed my mind. "Is this your first time with Seth?"

She hesitated before grinning. "No, and don't you dare tell Michael! He would be furious!"

Forget Michael, Caleb would be beyond furious if he knew. At least I wasn't the only one in the doghouse. "So, what's he like?" Virgin me knew nothing, but Seth seemed so knowledgeable. So did Grace, even if she didn't act like she was.

"Mmmm... Excellent! Very thorough and *very* enjoyable!" She glanced at me and then back to the road. "You and Michael still haven't?"

"No." I thought back to that morning, and how mad Michael had seemed. Combined with the mark that I was sure would make him run away from me screaming, it felt like we were probably never going to.

"I think I am going to need to be mated with someone like Seth." Grace must have sensed something was up and threw me a curve ball.

I laughed as I pressed my hands against my cheeks. "I wouldn't tell Michael or Caleb *that,* I'm pretty sure both of them would tear Seth apart!"

"I'm not interested in Seth, just someone like him – or at least with his qualities in the bedroom department!" She laughed her Tinkerbelle laugh, the mischief still in her eyes. "One day you are going to understand what I mean." She shot a glance at my shoulder. "The beast inside needs to be released and satisfied."

I stared at her wide eyed. Did she mean the Grollic in me? She knew about the birthmark on my shoulder blade but if I was a Grollic it would have been just below my collarbone and I hadn't turned into a Grollic on my eighteenth birthday. So, we effectively had no idea what it meant. Or was she just teasing me about my lack of experience and I'd turn into a beast once I had a taste for it?

Thankfully the school came into sight. I pushed the thoughts out of my mind as we pulled into our usual parking spot and then made our way towards the gymnasium. Students, faculty and family were arriving at the same time. Rushing, we made our way to find our cap and gowns on the racks inside the gym. Grace found hers and brought them to me.

"I'll be right back; I just need to do something for a moment. Can you hold my gown and cap?"

"Sure, where are you going?"

Grace leaned in and whispered, "Going to put your diploma beside mine so we can sit together and receive our diplomas together. I'll be right back, no one will notice me. Scouts honor." She held up two fingers and then walked out of the gym. She returned shortly after, and winking at me as she put her cap and gown on. "Good to go."

I laughed as not even a hair had been misplaced from her perfectly styled head.

"Attention students," Ms. Graid picked up her microphone "Can everyone get into alphabetical order so we could head into the auditorium? The graduation ceremony will be commencing in ten minutes."

Grace took my hand and led me to line up to the right of her. Then she scratched her head, and switched me to the other side. In single file the students made their way to their spots inside the auditorium that was already full of parents, family and friends.

I twisted in my seat, trying to find Michael. It seemed near impossible amidst the sea of faces behind us. "Do you know where...?" I asked Grace suddenly afraid the argument this morning would stop him from coming.

She sat quiet and then turned to look to her left. I followed her direction. Sarah stood up and waved in our direction, about ten rows back from us. Michael sat beside but there was no sign of Caleb. I didn't care, my only focus was on the blond blue eyed boy who smiled at me. The pendant around my neck warmed against my skin.

The vice president of the school came on stage and began speaking to everyone. Several teachers and coaches stood up to make speeches, and finally the President began calling the graduates names. Grace and I cheered as Simon stood on stage to accept his diploma; he turned and opened his gown to reveal a hot pink Speedo underneath with a Superman S painted on his chest. The auditorium erupted in laughter.

I waited for Damon's name to be mentioned. Guilt washed over me that no one seemed to notice his absence, believing he had left school or moved. He had kidnapped and planned to kill me. Instead, he was lying on the bottom of the lake near Caleb's cottage. He had attacked me in Grollic form, but I had no idea if his body would ever be found, and if it was, if it would still be in werewolf form.

"Rouge Thomas." A voice called over the loud speaker, followed by Grace Nightly. I couldn't stop myself from grinning as we stood. Grace had gotten our seats mixed so we quickly switched around as we walked up the aisle towards the stage. We shook hands and accepted our diplomas, and walked off stage...feeling nothing. This massive moment I had been waiting so long for didn't feel so monumental. It kind of felt like... no big deal. What a let-down.

As we walked off stage, Simon let out a loud whistle. I looked at Sarah and Michael who were clapping politely. Sarah held up her camera so Grace and I leaned in together for the far away photo. As we walked to the side of the stage, I tried to figure out why I was disappointed. I did feel a sense of liberty as I took my diploma and joined the rest of the graduates. I tried to drum up some excitement. This was it! I was free! The last string that had held me to the system had been cut. I was now officially free to move about the world!

Except all I wanted to do was head back to the pool house and read Bento's wolf book.

After what seemed like forever, everyone had received their diplomas, the President of the school introduced us officially, as graduates. We all moved our tassels to the other side of our hats and then threw them up in the air as the audience clapped. It was silly. Everyone around me laughed and hugged each other. I should be doing the same thing. All the people I loved were here to share it with me. I tried not to check my while standing beside Grace as she hugged classmates and joined in on photos.

We were dismissed to the gymnasium to meet with family and friends. Michael and Sarah were already inside the gymnasium when we walked in. I momentarily wondered how they had beat most of the crowd of parents, but quickly squashed the thought as the method was quite obvious. Sarah gave Grace a quick hug and handed her a little box. She turned to me and hugged me tightly.

"Congratulations dear." She kissed me on the forehead as she handed me a larger present. "Don't bother opening it now. It's a picture frame to put your diploma in. Thought you might like to hang it up."

"Thank you Sarah, that was very sweet of you." I hugged her before turning to Michael. I'd hidden behind Grace when we walked in because I suddenly felt shy and uncomfortable. Whatever had happened that morning had changed something between us. I had no idea how to get back to the way we had been. I slowly brought my gaze to his face.

In one motion he stepped toward me and swooped me into his arms, swinging me around. He set me down and grinned. "Congrats!" He handed me a small box.

"Open it now, Rouge!" Grace leaned over my shoulder to see.

I lifted the lid. Inside lay a lovely silver pocketknife inside. I lifted it up and turned it over to see it. There was a sterling mark and an inscription.

It read: *Freedom – the opportunity to choose... all my love Michael*

"It's beautiful Michael, thank you."

A quick smile crossed his lips. "I'd planned to have a card to show that your university courses would be paid for but I when I called to see what courses you were taking at the registrar's office, they said you weren't enrolled."

Crap. That was supposed to be something we would talk about as we headed out East. I swallowed and glanced at Grace's surprised face. "I was going to tell you, I just hadn't... yet." I looked down at the pocketknife in my hand.

Grace squeezed in between me and Michael. She put her arms around both of us. "Can we talk about this later? Maybe we could just celebrate the moment?"

Sarah squeezed my hand. "You kids enjoy yourselves, I'm going to head back to the house and meet up with Caleb." She nodded at Michael and Grace before heading to the exit.

Awkward silence followed as we watched her leave. I took a deep breath and exhaled it slowly, prepared to argue with Michael a second time that day if I had to.

Simon came running over and jumped in front of the three of us wearing a pair of sneakers, his gown flapping open to show off the Speedo and superman S on his chest. It was impossible not to laugh as he'd now tied his gown to look like a cape. He gave Grace a big hug and when he noticed the look on Michael's face, proceeded to shake my hand. I laughed and leaned in to hug him. He gave me a quick squeeze back but then released me. "Sorry, Michael. Not trying to hone in on your girl."

Grace swatted him on the back of the head. "Michael's only joking. That's his look all the time." I heard her mutter, "Miserable. Like Caleb."

If I heard that, Michael had definitely heard it.

"When are you heading down to Florida?" Grace asked Simon.

"About three weeks. I figured I might as well learn how to surf before I get to university. My folks bought me a surfboard for graduation! I have the coolest parents in the world!"

I saw Michael raise an eyebrow. "Way to go. That's fantastic you are continuing your education." He glanced at me from the corner of his eye. "Where are you going? University of Miami? What do you planning on studying?"

Simon waved his hand. "I didn't even try for one of the big schools. I'm going to get into hotel management. I got this cool job at a flashy hotel down in Miami. I get to do a lot of hopping and I think my Dad said I'll have to ring a huge brass bell. He keeps laughing when he's talking about it. Probably can't handle the fact that I'm going."

Michael nodded and kept his smile very tight. I, on the other hand, had to turn away so Simon wouldn't see my face. I didn't want to laugh at him, he was the biggest sweetie in the world, but he definitely wasn't the sharpest tool in the shed. I should have enrolled in the same courses. Then Michael wouldn't hound me for choosing to take a year off. I had enough on my plate at the moment.

"That's great Simon!" Grace hugged him. "I wish you loads of success and I hope you have tonnes of fun down in Miami!" She didn't care what he planned on doing, as long as he was happy.

"Let's go get our picture taken by the photo guy the school hired." He grabbed Grace's hand, leaving Michael and I alone.

We watched them go.

Michael finally broke the silence. "He's a... unique guy."

"Good thing Grace never brought him home to meet Caleb."

Michael glanced at me and then chuckled. He put his arm around my shoulder and pulled me close. "Probably a smart idea."

The awkward air between us disappeared. Either I could sense it, or the Sioghra pendant told me. I wasn't sure which, but it didn't matter, we were going to get through whatever was to come – together.

Chapter 8

Michael, Grace and I walked from the gymnasium to the front doors of the school one last time. I didn't feel the need to look back, that part of my life was finished and I had spent the evening sort of celebrating it with the two most important people in my life. I was ready to start on the next journey. We were headed to Grace's car, when I felt Michael slow his walk and my hand fall out of his.

"Sorry ladies, but there is *no way* that I am going home in *that* little lemon of a car!'

"It's not a lemon!' Grace stomped her foot, her hands going directly to her hips.

He grinned. "I call it like I see it.' He handed me his jacket. "You two drive back and I'll walk.'

"It'll take you over an hour to get back to the house if you walk!' I couldn't help but laugh at his refusal to get into the car. "I didn't know you had macho–issues.'

"Not for me.' He turned to Grace "Do you want to race?'

"Depends... am I racing you with the car? Or are we racing and letting Rouge drive the car back?' She was already slipping her shoes off and tossing them into the back seat.

"Rouge, you interested in making a small wager? Can you drive the car back on your own?' Michael undid his tie and tossed it into the back of the car.

"Seriously? You guys are nuts! What if someone sees you?'

"No one will.'

Grace taunted me, "Come on Rouge, who are you going to put the money on? Me, your best friend, or Michael?'

I was curious to see if they would beat me home and was tempted to offer my part in the race. I kept my mouth shut because I knew that there was no way Michael would risk any danger in my driving fast or reckless. "You guys have done this before, haven't you?'

"Loads.'

"Who usually wins?'

"Me,' they both said at the same time.

"Guess there's only one way to prove it then. How long is it going to take you to get to the house?'

"About ten minutes.' Michael answered.

"It's going to take me fifteen minutes to get home! I won't be able to judge who wins.' Guess I'd be playing on the safe side of the track and not racing them. The little car didn't stand a chance.

"We'll give you a five minute head start, or whatever you need. Just beep the horn twice, a long beep and then a short one. We'll heart it. That'll be the starting gun for us.'

Only a pair of idiots would want to have a race like that! I rolled my eyes at both of them, but got into the car. I actually wanted to see who would win. I knew Michael was really fast, but Grace had to be pretty close or Michael wouldn't have offered to race.

I rolled down the window as I drove by them. "See you crazy fools back at the house.' I kept checking my mirrors as I drove, positive I would see them come rushing by. I hurried and finally beeped the horn when I pulled onto their street. I parked the Beetle at the front of the long drive and got out of the car to wait. Leaning against the bumper I checked my watch. About six more minutes.

I stretched and rotated my shoulders. I planned on calling it a night when they got back. If we wanted an early start tomorrow, I needed to finish packing. Michael would head to his room to pack and while he was there, I would look at the Wolf Journal.

The mark on my back burned at the thought. I reached to try and touch it, knowing I wouldn't be able to.

A breeze picked up and blew my hair away from my face.

Vlko Dlak.

The word popped into my head and I shook my head. Where had that come from? I wrapped my arms around myself, chilled by strange feeling in my gut. *What the ...?*

"Wolf skin,' I said to myself. Vlko Dlak meant wolf skin. The marking on my back was Vlko Dlak. "No, dam it!' Another thought occurred to me that I didn't want to even think. I could stop it.

The Wolf Journal is made of wolf skin. I shook my head in disbelief but knew it was true. Why use leather from a cow when you could use the skin a wolf?

I checked my watch again. They should have been back about three minutes ago. I checked up and down the street but didn't see or hear anything. Maybe they had decided to make the race a little longer, or had added some obstacles along the way to make it more challenging. I looked one last time down the road and shrugged my shoulders.

It had grown cool and I wanted to see the Wolf Book at the pool house. They could let me know the winner when they got back.

I parked the car closer to the big house and then grabbed my diploma and frame from Sarah before locking the doors. Slipping my heeled shoes off, I jogged around the big house. I stopped short when I saw Michael and Grace sitting on the steps laughing together. I tossed my shoes in their direction – which they both easily ducked out of the way.

"I was waiting for you guys at the end of the driveway!'

Grace giggled. "We saw. Ran right by you. We were trying to guess how long it would take before you noticed us.'

"Breezed right by.' Michael blew out a breath and exaggerated the action with one fluid motion of his hand.'

"Who won then?'

"Tie.' Grace answered as Michael said, "I did.'

I looked at both of their faces. They looked like little kids. Both of them seemed so happy... so alive. It was hard to believe they were not as they appeared. I took a mental picture of the two of them; wanting to capture this moment forever. They probably had been quite competitive as children but never in a way that was negative; they would have encouraged each other to improve and been proud of who ever won. Their loyalty was their strongest bond and I suddenly had a feeling that was why they could communicate with each other. I smiled not wanting to break the moment. I could tell Michael what had happened later. "You two sit and hang out here, and if you don't mind, I am going to do some packing for the trip tomorrow. I have no idea what else I need to take along.'

"Would you like me to come in with you?' Michael asked, ever the gentleman.

"No, I'm fine.' I faked a yawn that turned into a real one. "I'm wiped. You should enjoy some time with your sister. Who knows how long we'll be away.'

Grace stomped her feet. "I should just come with the two of you.'

"No!' Michael and I said at the same time.

Grace shot me a knowing smile.

I had the decency to blush.

She stood and hugged me. "Just call if you need me. I'll be on the next plane.' She squeezed me tighter, trapping my breath in my chest. The frame slipped from my hand and fell to the ground, leaning against my leg. "Be careful.' She let go of me and stepped back.

I exhaled and sucked in a deep breath. "I will. Michael'll make sure of that.'

"I know. Otherwise I would be going.' She moved to let me up the few stairs of pool house. "I'll see you in the morning before you go.'

"'Night.' I leaned down and kissed Michael on the lips. The softness of his mouth warmed my skin. I closed my eyes and inhaled his delicious aftershave.

"I'll be in in a bit.' He kissed me again.

"Rouge?'

I was half way through the door and turned back to see what Grace wanted.

"Congratulations on graduating. I know this means a lot to you and I'm happy that I was able to share the moment with you.'

I smiled and winked at her; afraid if I said anything my voice might betray my feelings. Michael pointed to himself and held up two fingers. Then he put his palm to his face and blew a kiss my way. I pretended to catch it and pull it to my heart. I turned back, letting the screen door close quietly behind me.

I could hear the two of them talking very quietly. I couldn't make out any of the words as they talked extremely low and in a kind of short-hand – the gift of being what they were or the ability of twins. I couldn't be sure which.

I changed into comfortable pj's and headed to the bathroom to brush my teeth. After, I packed the rest of my toiletries and the last remaining things I needed for the next day. My diploma could be framed when we got back. I yawned and began flipping the lights off before crawling onto Michael's side of the bed. Leaving only the small lamp on beside the futon, I set the pillows so I could sit up.

The Wolf Book lay beside the bed waiting for me. I took a deep breath, glanced outside. Michael and Grace must have gone to the house as the little porch was empty now. I grabbed the journal and opened to the first entry in the book. I stared at the cursive writing a long moment before finally reading it.

March 1860.

I, Bentos, seventh son of Louis, have learned a most horrific family secret. I am from a family of shape-shifters – Grollics. Ugly, terribly ugly wolves. I am beyond words on how to explain. That is not the terrible secret.

I have known that for seventeen years. I have also known I am not one of them.

My six older brothers and father are all shape-shifters. However, today I learned that I am special – or so my father Louis tells me. As his seventh son, he named me Bentos to prevent the changing in me. It is a gift, he said, that I should be free of the curse. I was the one that could protect our family secret – the seventh child or son had the possibility to be free. He gave me that gift.

It is no gift. It is a curse! I am left without power and am weak. I have six brothers who mock my frailty and weakness. I am cursed to be a wretched man with no supremacy.

Or so I thought. Today on my seventeenth birthday, my anger overtook my reason as I broke my fast. Charles, my eldest brother, sat mocking my misfortune, laughing at my weakness. Today, as I turned seventeen, I should have had the transformation. It would not happen because of the gift my father bestowed on me. I am tired of feeling weak when I know that inside of me, I am brilliant and strong of mind.

I have power inside of me that is fuelled upon the anger that festers in my soul.

I stood up, defiant of Charles, and challenged him. He laughed at my defiance and said I needed to learn the lesson of humility – to be put in my place. I stepped around the table as my father came in to stop the argument. Charles turned into a horribly ugly beast and charged at me. Father could do nothing to stop him.

I knew if he reached me, death would be my friend. I hated him beyond reason for having what should have been mine.

Inside I broke, and silent thunder erupted from me. It shook the house, and I screamed for Charles to die that instant.

Suddenly Charles lay dead at my feet.

My brothers rushed in as my father screamed. They saw Charles and grew angry at what I had done. They cursed me and said I had made a pact with the devil in turn for Charles' blood. They rose together and shifted into Grollics.

I begged them to stop but they would not listen.

I forced them to stop. Lo and behold, the tide has shifted. I am no longer a servant of the beast. They are mine to do with as I please.

Father was terrified at what I had done. I set my brother Andrew to kill him and mother. He attacked and father did nothing to protect himself.

Who is the weak one now, Father?

My mocking brothers are now slaves, set to do my bidding.

I have this power over the Grollic beast that I must learn to the best of my abilities. I will educate myself on all the strengths this gift possesses and conquer all.

I will find any and all weaknesses of these terrible wolves. I will journal all I know about them – to kill, to fear me, and my power.

I hate the Vlko Dlak with a terrible venom.

I will use them as slaves until they are nothing, and I have everything.

Bentos

I stared at the hand written confession, because that's what it was: a century-and-a-half-old confession. My head shook at the maniac who was the author of this journal. Bentos had been jealous of his brothers and angered at his own weakness. He had killed his family. He had been a horrible person who craved power and he'd done terrible things with it. Someone that power hungry? He must have wanted to control Michael and Grace's kind when he found out about them. How did he even know they existed?

I slammed the journal shut and tossed it on floor by my backpack. I had read enough.

I hated Grollics like he had, but I was not him. Whatever Bentos was, I would *never* become. I swore it.

Chapter 9

Early the next morning I woke on my side of the bed with Michael quietly sitting beside me.

"Did you sleep alright?' Michael murmured as his hand caressed my cheek.

I smiled and rolled over to stretch, enjoying the vision I had the pleasure of waking up to. "What time did you and Grace finally say good night?' I tried to remember what time I had fallen asleep.

"I came in here about twenty minutes ago actually. Grace is sitting out on the step writing a list of for us.'

"A list?' Humans wrote lists " list for groceries, lists for packing, and anything else we thought we might forget. Grace and Michael didn-t need to write lists, they remembered everything.

Michael rolled his eyes. "It-s a list of topics for us to discuss on the road so we don-t get bored. I think she-s also making up some road games for us to play.' He was trying not laugh, speaking quietly so Grace wouldn-t hear him.

I smiled at the thought of Grace drumming a pencil to a pad of paper as she tried to come up with ideas for us. It was her way of being in the car without doing the road trip. "It sounds like a great idea. Grace is awesome!' I said it loud so she would hear. I winked at Michael. I jumped out of the bed and headed towards the bathroom before he could make a comment.

I used to have short showers while living with my foster parents, just one of their endless attempts to suck any form of joy out of my life; and oddly enough, even though I now lived pretty much in the lap of luxury, the short shower routine had still stuck with me. However, today I spent extra time enjoying the hot water. I had no idea if we were driving straight through or staying in hotels along the way, so no way of knowing when I might next have the pleasure of a hot shower. I had left all the travel planning to Michael, so I could concentrate on school. After the shower, I dressed in a pair of thin pants and a red tank top, figuring comfort on the road was more important than looking fashionable. Besides, what did I know about looking fashionable? I blow-dried my hair as quickly as I could and added threw on some mascara, my only real concession to my more "girly' inclinations.

Dressed and ready, I headed to pack a few last things into my backpack. On the coffee table, sat a Starbucks latte. I offered a thank you to whichever caring soul had sought to sooth my need for caffeine.

Grace came strolling in with her list, tossing it onto the table as she sat down.

"Are you all packed?' she asked.

"Pretty much. I was thinking I should fill a cooler with some food.'

"Good idea. Michael gets crabby if he doesn-t snack.' She watched me a few moments, inhaling a sharp breath when I picked up the wolf book and my journal.

"Everything okay?'

She shifted in her seat. "With me or with you?'

I gave her a questioning look, trying to stuff my defensiveness back into its black hole in my head. I was getting tired of all the weird questioning from the Thompson family. It wasn-t Grace-s fault, but I couldn-t stop myself. "I-m totally fine. Great in fact! What-s your problem?' I hated the irritation in my voice but didn-t apologize.

Grace stood, crossing her arms over her chest. "Michael told me about the wolf book. You can read another part again? How do you feel?' She tapped her back, referring to my birthmark. "Do you *feel* any different?'

I zipped up my backpack roughly. "Did you say something to Michael?'

Grace shook her head.

I sighed. "Sorry. I just... I don't know. I'm anxious about the book, about travelling and what we are going to find out. Caleb's irritated with me. It seems Michael's annoyed. I just want things to be normal.'

"Normal? That flew out the window a long time ago.'

"Doesn't mean a girl can't dream.'

Grace laughed. "You're going to be okay. Michael's with you.' She hugged me, squeezing me tight. "I'm a phone call away if you need me. Remember that.' She leaned in and whispered, as if afraid someone might hear, "Just don't keep too many secrets. They weigh you down.'

Didn't she realize? That was why I was going. I hoped to find some answers. "I'll miss you.'

"Me, too.' Grace let go of me just as Michael came through the door. "Call me.'

"I will.'

"Or I'll bug Michael and use him as a phone.' She ruffled her brother's hair as she ran by him. "Chat soon, big bro.'

Michael watched her go with wide eyes. "What'd I do now?'

"Nothing!' she called back, nearly at the house.

He shook his head and turned to me and grinned. "You ready?'

"Almost. Just want to empty the fridge into a cooler for us.'

Michael had the back of the Jeep packed and organized by the time I had finished the kitchen and tidied the pool house. While he left to load the cooler into the Jeep, I had one last walk around. I couldn't help but feel a sense of change, the feeling that had been missing during graduation. It bothered me that I was so apprehensive about the future and that I would miss this place so much; that the next time I came back here things would be very different. I was worried the cloud I felt over my head wasn-t just common, every-day bad luck, but more a sense of doom about what I would learn about myself. All I wanted was answers. How could that leave me with such a sense of foreboding?

Michael came back to the pool house, to find me standing at the entrance. He stood silently beside me for a few moments, and then put his cool hand into mine. "Rouge, whatever happens, whatever you learn, it-s the *past*. It-s not who you are right now, who you spent the last eighteen years discovering. It isn-t going to change who you are inside. You-ll still be you " the girl who I love, and who, strangely enough, just happens to know how to talk to wolves.' He squeezed my hand and led me outside.

We walked around to the front of the house where the Jeep sat parked beside Grace-s little Beetle.

Sarah was waiting by the cars for us. She came over the moment she saw us. "I hope you find what you-re looking for.' She hugged me and said nothing more. She waved to Michael.

"Thanks, we-ll see you soon and let you know if we find anything.'

She nodded and headed inside.

I went around to the passenger-s side of the jeep. Caleb stood leaning against the door. I had hoped he wouldn-t be around to see us off, but there was no avoiding him now.

"Hello Caleb,' I said trying to appear indifferent.

I stood awkwardly, not sure what to say or do when he didn-t reply.

Michael broke the silence, "Caleb, I-ll see you in a week.'

A week? Hadn-t we planned to be away for three or four weeks?

Caleb nodded and moved to open the door for me. "Let me know if you learn anything important from the book. If you are able to figure out a way to decode it, have Michael call me. I-m sure whatever you learn will help us—I mean you, it will help you.' He leaned over to speak directly to Michael already inside the Jeep. "Watch yourself. I-ll send Seth, just say the word.

That set off my internal alarm bells. Something was up. And it had nothing to do with me. I resolved to get answers out of Michael as soon as we were on our way.

He closed my door and walked toward the house. It was June and he still wore a long tan coat, its tails flapping in the wind behind him. He still had the presence of a seventeenth century lord and often dressed the part. The interesting bit was that it suited him and made him look very classy, instead of ridiculous. I hated myself for being fascinated and terrified of him at the same time.

Michael started the Jeep and drove down the driveway towards the road. He handed me the GPS. "I put some maps under your seat if you want to follow them.'

"What-s Caleb concerned about? Has there been any trouble?' I watched his face, searching for some clue to show he might be hiding something. "The wolf kind?'

Michael looked at me and then turned his eyes back on the road. "There have been a few problems along the south-east coast. It seems that there is a pack of wolves that have been attacking a number of cities. They are obviously looking for something or someone, but Caleb, I mean the Higher Coven, is unsure of what, or who. It is nothing to worry about, as a few scouts have been sent out to try and determine what the problem is. It has nothing to do with us.'

By the carefully neutral tone of his voice, I immediately knew it was a much bigger deal than he was making it out to be, but I didn-t push him to tell me more. We had a long drive ahead of us. He-d talk about it when he was ready.

As we pulled onto the highway and drove away from Port Coquitlam, Michael began to talk. "Did you read any of the Bentos–journal last night?'

I leaned over the seat and grabbed my backpack. Pulling the Wolf book out, I set it on my lap. "I did. Let me read it to you.' I read the passage I had read last night out loud. When I was done, I sat quietly for a moment, waiting for some reaction. When none came, I asked, "What do you think of him?'

"Madman. He was evil the day I met him. All he wanted was power and control. That wasn-t something learned. It sounds like he was like that since he could think and reason.' He took one hand off the wheel to squeeze mine. "You may have his gift, but everything else in you was given to you by your mother.'

I wanted so desperately to believe him. However, there was a part of me, hidden deep inside, that screamed for that power that Bentos had written about. I had spent so much of my life powerless to control what happened to me, like Bentos had. I feared that it might one day consume me as it had done to Bentos, and then, I would be no better than him. The only thing I had that Bentos had lacked, was love. Michael had shown me how to love, and how to be loved. Whatever was going to happen, he would never leave me. Bentos had no understanding of that concept.

We headed down the main highway that would take us out of the State, on our route towards the east. I slid the Wolf Book under the seat and pulled out my journal so I could write.

Note to Self:

Michael and I have started our journey across the country back to where I assume I was born. It seems a lifetime ago that I lived in Niagara Falls, and that I was so angry about leaving. Amazing how things can change when your eyes are opened. Aside from this year, I feel like I have spent the rest of my 18 years inside a dark cloud, never looking towards the sun. Words cannot express how I feel about Michael; he has brought life back into this dead body. I AM ALIVE NOW!

I read the first entry in Bentos' journal. He's a terrible person. I'm scared I may become like him. He talks of the hatred inside of him for the wolf and I understand that feeling. I feel it deep inside of me, like a burn that is a fire trying to break through. I have tried to forget and avoid thinking about it since that awful day in January when it started. I've pretended it didn't happen for the past six month. I'm tired of pretending. I want those beasts out of my life!

I'm terrified it is going to consume and change who I am. It's just too much to worry about right now, so I just want to get to Niagara Falls, find out what I can about my past and get some closure. Maybe by getting these answers, I'll gain some insight or some kind of tool, to help me keep control of myself, to make sure that dark part of me never sees the light of day.

I wonder if either of my parents know that I'm still alive. If they are, do they care? What became of them? I'm 18 now so my records are no longer sealed. I'll be able to find out their names, and then find out where they live. It's both an exciting and a terrifying thought.

Rouge

Chapter 10

The drive across the country flew by. We decided to drive straight through, Michael resting a bit during the day if he felt he needed it, and letting me sleep through the night. He drove like a maniac, but with his special talents, he had no problem staying under the radar of police or avoiding causing any accidents. The trip took us fifty hours, and that was only because Michael insisted that we stop so I could stretch and we could eat. While it felt incredibly long, it was still a lot more fun than the trip with Jim and Sally the previous year from Niagara Falls to Port Coquitlam.

Early Monday afternoon we pulled onto interstate ninety that would take us through Buffalo and onto Niagara Falls. I recognized all the landmarks I had grown up with, and began shifting and moving in my seat as we neared, getting antsier by the moment.

"You excited?" Michael had been very quiet the last hour, but had been constantly glancing at me.

"Yeah—No, actually. I feel kinda nervous. I'm sorta wishing we were back in Port Q." I bit my lip and looked at him. "Please tell me this was a good idea – that I haven't made a mistake in wanting to come here?"

His hand reached for mine and held it. "I don't think this is a mistake at all. Trust your instincts, they're usually right."

We headed towards the tollbooth and bridge for Grand Island. The large, blue, twin bridges has always seemed beautiful to me.

Now they looked like mountains I was going to have to climb. We drove through Grand Island in silence. I had nothing to say because my mind was running through everything that had happened in the past year, while I was trying to remember my first memories from when I was little. I couldn't come up with anything significant. The twin blue bridges appeared again to take us into Niagara Falls. I pointed to the Niagara Boulevard exit. "We can find a hotel here if you want."

"Sure. Good idea." He pulled into the right lane and then headed onto the exit ramp. He headed south on the boulevard. A couple miles down, past all the shops and restaurants was a brand new Holiday Inn that advertised an Indoor + Outdoor pool on its welcome sign. He parked the car under the entrance by the office. "Give me a sec to grab us a room."

I waited in the car, rubbing my temples with my fingers, trying to get myself to relax. I tried concentrating on my breathing and counted even numbers until my racing heart slowed and I began to feel calm. I took one more deep breath and looked up as Michael walked around the Jeep and got into the driver's seat.

"We are on the first floor, just around the corner. Let's get our stuff inside and grab some lunch."

"Good idea. I'll give my old Foster-Counsellor a call and see if I can set up a meeting for tomorrow. Mrs. Hawthorn always left Tuesday mornings open for kids who needed to see her without an appointment. I'm pretty sure she won't have a problem with me coming in."

Mrs. Hawthorn had been my guidance-foster counsellor before I had moved to Port Coquitlam. She was a woman who would do nothing without your case file in front of her. She was a good lady, just beaten down by years with the system.

We walked into the hotel room and threw our bags down. Michael went back to the Jeep and made a few trips with the rest of our stuff. He flopped down onto the king size bed. I dropped down beside him – he on his back and me on my belly. I folded my arms across his chest and rested my chin between my hands.

"So... is there anything you would like to do?" I leaned my face closer to his and my lips brushed lightly against his as I spoke. I'd brushed my teeth and freshened up while he ran back and forth to unload.

"Hmmm... I can't seem to think of anything at the moment." He brought his hands from behind his head and rested them along my ribcage. Ever so gently, he pulled me so I lay on top of him.

I brought my lips towards his neck and nibbled my way to his ear. I heard him sigh, and it gave me courage. I brushed my hand across his chest and undid a few of his buttons. His skin was cool but it created heat inside of me as I ran my fingers along his abdominal muscles. I brought my lips towards his and felt his tongue instantly inside of my mouth. I groaned and pressed my body closer to his.

In a flash, Michael flipped us so he was on top of me. It only created more burning heat inside. I opened the remaining buttons on his shirt and ran my hands over his chest and stomach. It was intoxicating.

His hands pulled at my shirt. His mouth never left mine as his hands touched my stomach and reached higher towards my breasts. I wanted this, badly. A desire burned inside me that I had never felt before. I broke away from his kiss so I could sit and pull my shirt off.

The moment our lips parted and before I had time to sit all the way up, Michael was on the other side of the room. I sat frozen in surprise, my hands crisscross, fingers holding the bottom of my shirt. "Why did you..."

He face tightened as he struggled to gain his composure. His chest heaved ad he was pressed up against the wall as if trying to disappear into it. His eyes were the deepest blue I had ever seen them. He shut them tight and clenched his hands into fists by his side.

"Michael –"

"Please... Rouge, give me a moment. I just need a moment."

"Is something wrong?" I had no clue what had happened. Was he reacting this way because of me? Had Grace sent him a terrible message? "What's going on?" I stood and walked over. "Is everything alright?"

He nodded curtly, his eyes still closed tight.

When I reached him, I put both my hands on top of his clenched fists. I didn't move, I just stood there until I could feel his hands begin to relax. I laced my fingers into his and watched his face. He slowly opened his eyes to look at me. They were still blue, but a much lighter shade. I leaned forward and stood on my tippy toes to rub my nose against his.

He smiled, his body still pressed tight against the wall.

"Are you okay?"

He nodded.

"What happened? Did Grace send you a message?" Their uncanny ability to talk to each other inside their heads never ceased to amaze me. "Is everyone alright back in Port Q?" With my luck a pack a Grollics attacked the day we left.

He chuckled. "No. I mean yes." He shook his head. "Everyone's fine. It wasn't Grace."

"Then what happened?"

He grinned but avoided looking me in the eye.

I stood on my tippy toes, trying to catch his gaze.

His fingers left mine and trailed up my side and across my collarbone to the pendant around my neck. "I think it came from this."

"What? What came from it?" I had no idea what was going on. "Did I shock you or something?"

"In a sense." He smirked. "I'm not exactly sure if it came from the pendant."

"Did *I* shock you? What the heck happened?" I couldn't stop the frustration from entering my voice.

"We were... kissing. One moment our lips were pressed against each other, the next... Wham! I felt everything you were feeling. Like this massive balloon of desire coursed through you and burned into me. It was..." He smiled, one very sexy smile. "Incredible. It was unbelievably incredible. Could you do it again?"

I grinned, but shook my head. "I've no idea what I did."

"You didn't feel it?"

"I'm not sure. I mean, I was..." I whispered the next word, embarrassed but didn't know what other word to use, "horny. But I didn't try to send you any feeling." My fingers curled around the Sioghra. "Maybe it was the pendant."

He leaned close and pressed his lips softly against mine. "We'll have to see if you can do it again."

A tingling burned deep in my belly. "Now?"

He smiled wryly, taking a deep breath. "How 'bout we eat something first."

"Are you feeling light headed and faint?" I teased.

He looked at me with that sexy-smile that always melted my heart. "In a totally new way." He tickled my ribs.

I jumped away, laughing. "Let me give Mrs. Hawthorn a shout before we go. Then let's drive down to the Falls and do some sightseeing. My legs are dying to walk around after being stuck in the Jeep for so long."

"Sounds perfect."

I pulled Mrs. Hawthorn's card out of my backpack and dialed her number.

"Hello?"

"Mrs. Hawthorn?"

There was a pause on the phone. "Rouge?"

"Yes!" I smiled. She remembered me. "I'm in town and was wondering if I could stop by and see you? I know you used to keep

Tuesday morning's open..."

Paper shuffled and a filing cabinet clicked shut in the background. "I have one appointment now and will be done in about forty minutes. Why don't you came by in an hour?"

"Today?" I hadn't expected to see her today.

"If that works for you."

"Sure. I'll see you in an hour." I looked at Michael whose eyebrows shot up in surprise.

"See you then." Mrs. Hawthorn hung up before I had a chance to say good-bye.

Michael checked his watch. "She can see you today?"

"I guess so." I stood and grabbed the duffle bag I'd packed my clothes in. "I need to jump in the shower. I'll be super quick."

Michael knocked on the door as I turned the water on. "I'm going to go and grab us some food. I'll find a drive-through of some kind."

"Okay. Thanks!" I called out.

When I walked out of the bathroom fifteen minutes later, Michael sat at the desk, talking on his cell phone giving the address of our hotel with the room number. "Check the area and let me know what you find out."

"Caleb?" I asked when he hung up.

"Yup." He pointed to the dresser. "I just grabbed a sub. Wasn't sure what else to get."

"That's fine." I straightened my skirt. "I'm not that hungry actually. Maybe I'll wait till after."

"Eat a little. Please?"

Not wanting to show my anxiousness, I unwrapped the sub and took a small bite. "Why did you ask Caleb to check the area?"

"I don't know how many Grollics are in the area. Caleb was looking into it. It's not really something we have on a file. There are no Higher Coven members in this area so Grollics might be here because of that – or they may not be here for a completely different reason. I just don't want to tick anyone off because I didn't respect their squatter's rights."

"Squatter's rights?"

"It is kind of like in real estate – you settle on a piece of land long enough, you kind of own it. I need to know the area better before I take any initiative. It's not a big deal." He picked up his empty sub wrap and tossed it into the bin. "Just not everyone is a fan of the Higher Coven."

"Should I be worried?" I hadn't thought about Michael's safety. My focus had been on finding answers about my past. Guilt washed over me. I'd been so selfish.

"No. We're just being cautious." He grabbed the keys and tossed them to me. "You know where to go?"

I nodded.

Michael opened the room door. As we headed down to the car, he made an effort to distract me. "Sarah told me we have to go to Fort George and see Fort Niagara as well. She was here when they were built."

"She fought in the war of 1812?" Impressive.

"She actually helped the Canadians," Michael tapped his forehead. "I think he was actually English. Brock. His name was something Brock."

"*Sir* Isaac Brock?" I asked, my mouth gapping open.

"Yeah, that's it." Michael tried to hide a smile. He was obviously enjoying my disbelief.

I laughed as we got into the Jeep. "I'm so asking Sarah the details when we get back." I started the engine and pulled out of the parking lot. Twenty minutes later we were in front of the familiar Foster Care – Children Services building. I parked the Jeep in the visitors parking. We walked together into the building, Michael's warm hand holding mine. I gave my name to the secretary at the front desk and we sat in the chairs waiting for Mrs. Hawthorn to call me in.

Nothing had changed; the paint, the chairs, the pictures. Nothing here had changed, but to me, nothing looked the same.

Mrs. Hawthorn came out of her office, folder in hand. She looked up from her bifocals and called my name.

"Rouge dear, how are you? Oh, I see that you have brought a friend." She looked at Michael and began fanning her face with her hand. "What a lovely, handsome friend you have!" She shook her head, as if trying to figure if she had said the words aloud or in her head.

I smiled and tried not to laugh – I had the same feeling every day.

The three of us walked into her office, she still had files piled everywhere. She moved files from a chair and plopped them onto the floor by the wall. She sat down behind her desk and pointed to the pair of chairs for us to sit in. Michael held the first chair out for me and then sat himself down. Mrs. Hawthorn gave him a winning smile.

"Thanks for seeing me, Mrs. Hawthorn. Mrs. Hawthorn?" It took me calling her name twice to turn her attention back to me.

"Sorry Rouge." She folded her small hands together. "Why did you want to see me?"

"I was wondering if you would be able to give me a copy of my birth certificate from the hospital and any other information that might help me find my biological parents."

She tutted. "Oh dear, let me see." She opened the file in front of her and shuffled through the pages. "You turned eighteen back in January. So you are entitled to any information we might have about your birth. Let me what we have on file with our secretary. She'll be able to get a copy of what we do have." She stood and slipped out of the office leaving the door slightly open behind her.

As soon as she left, Michael was instantly behind her desk looking through my case file. I hadn't even seem him move.

"Michael! What're you doing?" I whispered.

"Just making sure sweet-ol' Mrs. Hawthorn doesn't leave anything out. Don't worry; she won't even know I looked." He flipped through each page at lightning speed. How he could read anything that fast was beyond me.

He was sitting down beside me before Mrs. Hawthorn even came back into the room.

"Rouge, here are the forms to apply for the original copy of your birth certificate. We only have a copy. Here also are the hospital papers when we retrieved you." Mrs. Hawthorn handed me a small stack of papers.

Retrieved me? What was that supposed to me?

Michael cleared his throat but Mrs. Hawthorn continued before he could speak.

"If you turn to the third page of the hospital notes and look on the left hand side, about mid-way down... you'll see that you were born six and a half, nearly seven weeks, prematurely and weighed just over 4lbs. You were actually born in Utica, New York." She skimmed through the photocopy on her desk, pushing her reading glasses up the bridge of her nose. "It's a little confusing. Doctor reports show you being here, but the birth was down there." She set the papers down. "Because you were so tiny, you were kept at the hospital in Utica for two and half months before being released."

"So I was just left there?" I tried sorting through the papers but couldn't seem to make heads or tails out of the doctor's notes and other pages. A few slipped out and drifted to the floor.

Michael leaned down to pick them up.

"Your pediatrician check-ups from three months to somewhere around thirty-six months are in Niagara Falls."

That made sense. If FACS picked me up then everything would have been done here. "Did my mother stick around to at least put her name on my birth certificate?"

"Stick around?" Mrs. Hawthorn's eyebrows rose. "I'm sorry, I thought you knew."

"Knew what?" Michael straightened beside me.

"Your mother left you at the hospital just after you were born and then came back when you were released."

"What?" I was sure I had never been told that. I definitely would have remembered it.

"She picked you up," Mrs. Hawthorn flipped to the front of my file. "The day FACS came, she showed up just before us and said she had changed her mind. She picked you up."

My heart stuttered and its beat pounded inside my ears. "Really?" I whispered.

"Yes. She had you till you were about three and then brought you back to Utica Hospital. She signed you over again to us... and this time she didn't come back."

Michael reached for my hand and held it tight in his.

"I thought I was with the system since I was born."

"Well, in a sense you were. You've been on file since your birth."

"What's my mother's name?" I stood and looked over Mrs. Hawthorn's file. "Do you have that?"

She leaned back against her chair, maybe surprised at my sudden movement. "She requested it not be released. When she handed you over the second time, she left written notice not to release her name." Mrs. Hawthorn smiled sadly. "I'm sorry. I don't have it."

We'd come all this way for nothing then.

"So," Michael said as he rose from his seat and stood beside me. "All you have for Rouge are the forms and what you've photocopied for her? Can't you give her your file?"

Mrs. Hawthorn's mouth dropped. "The file is state property! I can't do that."

"Psych evaluations, notes on her foster homes and all that crap is her business. Not the states." He crossed his arms over his chest. "Why don't you make photocopies and give Rouge the originals?"

Mrs. Hawthorn pointed a tiny finger at Michael. She obviously didn't take bullying from anyone. "You listen to me, young man!

I've been here a long time. If I could do that I would. Rouge doesn't need what's in this file. She needs to focus on moving forward with her life." She slapped the file shut and pounded her fist on top of it. "Let her do that."

I put my hand on Michael's to stop him. "Let's just go." I couldn't erase the image of what I had expected my mother to look like, fitting her into my internal fantasy, sitting, rocking me as a small baby and singing me to sleep. She had wanted me – at least for a little while. That would have to be enough... for now. "Thanks Mrs. Hawthorn."

She stood and walked with us to the lobby.

Michael felt the back pocket of his shorts. "Shoot! My wallet must have fallen out when I picked up the papers for you. I'll be right." He jogged back to Mrs. Hawthorn's office and disappeared. He was back a moment later, holding his wallet in the air. "Found it!"

We said good-bye and headed to the Jeep. I gave Michael the keys to drive. "Can we head back to the hotel?" I just wanted to sleep. I suddenly felt exhausted.

Michael pulled out of the parking lot and onto the main road. He leaned forward, close to the steering wheel.

"What are you doing?" I asked.

"Untuck my shirt will you?"

As I pulled it out of his shorts, I felt something hard on his back. "What the...?" His shirt came free and a manila envelope appeared.

"I figured this belongs to you."

I pulled the envelope out all the way, simply unable to believe what I found. "You stole my file?"

Chapter 11

I glanced behind us in the back window, expecting Mrs. Hawthorn to be chasing us with some flashing light taped to the top of her car. She probably drove some kind of car from the seventies, some huge hunker that she had to sit on a phone book just so she could see over the steering wheel. "I can't believe you stole it!"

"The information belongs to you. Do you want me to take it back?" Michael asked, glancing in the rear view mirror.

I turned around. "No!" It felt weirdly exhilarating and scary at the same time. I opened the file on my lap, but left it there, unable to look down.

"Do you want me to look at it?" Michael asked quietly.

I inhaled a deep breath and let it out slowly. "I'll do it. Just seems weird to have most of my life just sitting here." I felt protective of it, like I did with the Wolf Book. This was mine. In my whole life, almost nothing had been mine and mine alone. This...was my history, mine in a unique way, a way that made it impossible to for anyone to take it away from me once I knew it. The problem was, I wasn't sure I wanted to know, now that I had it all literally in my lap. I stared out the window for a moment, frozen in indecision. Wasn't this what I had made the trip for? Didn't I need to know this? It was mine. Mine. And yet, it wasn't. Not yet. The good news was though, that all I had to do to claim it, was to read it. Such a simple task, but one that was almost as hard to complete as making myself read the Wolf Book.

Ultimately, it was a bump in the road that made the decision for me. Michael couldn't avoid the pothole in the asphalt. The jeep bumped and the folder started to go flying. I had to plant my hands on my lap to keep everything from flying all over the place. It seemed like a sign. Whether it was subconscious, or a sign from On High, I didn't know. However, it was obvious that I wanted and needed to claim my history.

Lifting the left side, I let everything fall to the right so I could start at the beginning. There were some photocopies and notes. "You know what I don't believe?"

Michael glanced at me from the corner of his eye. "What?" He pulled down some scenic route and found a lookout point of the Niagara River. He put the Jeep in park and let the engine idle.

"I don't believe my birth mother ever kept me." I stared blankly at the file. "I mean, I would remember that, wouldn't I?" I dug through my earliest memories searching for some sign of her, even just a feeling of cared for, but there was nothing. Not a warm hug, kind word or anything that would let me think I had been loved.

"I don't know. I mean, if she left you before you were three, that's pretty early to remember."

"Why would she leave me in the hospital, then pick me up and then drop me off there again?" I couldn't wrap my head around it. I flipped through the first five or six pages of the file and came to a medical page with my vaccination history. The doctor was located in Niagara Falls. "It looks like I lived here and then she dropped me off in Utica. Why drive all that way down there to get rid of me." *Only to end up back here again.* "It just doesn't make sense."

"Maybe she thought she could keep you and then finically couldn't afford to."

"But she picked me up at the hospital the day I was supposed to be given away. That doesn't get her out of the medical bills."

"Okay. So maybe it wasn't about the money..." His let his sentence trail off.

I scanned a few more of the medical pages but most of it didn't make sense or simply held no importance, no key to who my mother was. "You think my father might not have wanted me?"

Michael pressed his lips together before finally speaking. "Maybe... and I am just saying maybe... maybe your mother already had a family. Maybe she met someone and had an affair."

It didn't sound true. I don't know why I didn't believe it; it was plausible after all. I just didn't. "No. I don't think that's it." My stomach churned at the next thought. "Maybe she got rid of me because I wasn't marked. She's probably a Grollic and came back to check if I had the birthmark by my collar bone." I reached for the spot that was smooth and without blemish. Like a bullet going straight through my body, the exact same spot on my back burned. Maybe she had seen the mark on my back and known what it meant. Maybe she had thrown me away because of it.

"Or she was raped by a Grollic and couldn't bear to look at you and the memory it brought back." I looked at him with horror written all over my face. Michael squeezed my shoulder. "That sounds terrible, but something dramatic must have happened. I can't imagine anyone giving you up."

It soothed the awful sense of revulsion that had instantly sprouted in my heart. He was sweet; one of the reasons I loved him so much. "I guess we need to find her and ask why then." I flipped back to the first pages looking for a name.

"It might not be that easy," Michael said quietly. "She requested that her information not be given to you when you were legal age. That's going to put a quite the bump in the research road."

I didn't hear him. I'd stop listening as I stared at the page in front of me. I tuned everything out but the words on the page. Slowly I handed it to him.

He looked at me, eyebrows raised.

"If you look on the right side, near the bottom, you'll see it."

He glanced down, lifted the page and tilted his head. He flipped back to the front and glanced at me.

"Ih-Ihh..." I cleared my throat and tried again, my voice coming out in a whisper, "My mother's signature."

Michael's head dropped down. "Ohhhhh... I see it."

"Rebekah. Her name's Rebekah Gnowee." I shrugged. "Or however you say it. I'm guessing there won't be too many of those in the phone book." I tapped my finger against my thigh. The last name sounded so weird. I planned to google it when I got back to the hotel later.

Michael set the Jeep into drive and pulled back onto the road. "Let's head back to the hotel and see what we can find." He tossed the file back onto my lap. "Is there an address on the page when she signed you over to the state?"

I ripped open the file folder to double check.

My heart nearly stopped. "There is... Holy crap! There is!" My hands shook at the address scrawled below the signature, her name printed and an apartment number in Niagara Falls.

"Put it in the GPS. Let's go there now."

"Now?" My heart that had felt like it has stopped a minute ago now felt like it was racing down a giant hill on a pair of roller skates. Michael was right. This is what I came here for. I tapped the address into the GPS. "Nothing like the element of surprise."

I was awkwardly trying to close keep pages from falling all over the place and enter the address into the GPS, when a folded sheet with hand written notes slipped out of the file. It read:

Utica Hospital

Baby Doe, aka Rouge (R), was born premature. Biological mother was in a terrible state when R was delivered. She left the hospital before being medically released and never signed the forms to hand her over to the state. Only left a note to say the infants name was to be Rouge. Then the woman up and left; disappeared. She came the day we released R to the state. Dr. Mormar was the attending physician. He asked this note be written in case baby R is returned to the state again.

"I wonder where I got the name Thomas from?" I said out loud.

"Maybe your biological mother gave you the name so it would be easier for her to find you."

I scoffed. "Thomas isn't that unique, you know. Gnowee would have definitely been easier to find."

"Okay then. Maybe she gave it to you because she was trying to hide you from someone."

"I doubt it. There's a note here that she left a note to say my name was Rouge. No last name. The state probably gave it to me. Jones, Smith, Thomas... something simple."

"Did you know that your name means *pure*?"

I have him an odd look. Had he looked it up? "Really? My last name?"

He shook his head. "Your first name." He made a left turn, following the GPS. "Maybe there's a reason why she named you that. Maybe she named you Rouge, in the hopes of keeping you pure from the past." He shrugged his shoulders, "Just trying to be a little philosophical for the moment."

I patted his shoulder and laughed. "You're doing a great job." I straightened and stared out the window, filled with a new sense of purpose and drive. "Okay. Let's go find my mom."

Chapter 12

It didn't take nearly as long as I had though it would before we were there. I had double-checked the address in the folder to the GPS. "This has to be it." The disbelief in my voice couldn't be missed. I wasn't expecting much, but this?

I bent my neck to get a better view through the Jeep window at the rundown apartment building. The neighborhood matched it a little too perfectly. I shivered. *If my mother kept me, this is where I would have lived.*

Michael sensed my thoughts. "She might have given you up because she wanted more for you than this." *Or she was hiding here.*

My head swiveled in his direction as I felt his thought. Touching the Sioghra, I had no idea if it had come from it or if I had simply made the thought sound as if it had come from Michael. "It's starting to feel like a super-long day. Maybe we should just head back and check a phone book or something." Michael looked at me with sympathy, understanding my urge to run away, and it made me want to be stronger.

I closed my eyes. "Sorry. It's fine. We need to do this. I'll be fine. I need to do this." I was rambling, trying to build courage and hide my anxiety. *You're doing a lousy job,* I told myself.

Michael pulled the jeep to the side of the curb. He didn't say anything, which only made me more nervous.

"Think we should go and try to find a phone number first?" I played with a corner of the paper, tearing little pieces off.

Michael cut the engine and stuffed the keys in his pocket. "What're you going to say if you call?"

I glanced out the window again to the third floor. Somewhere behind one of those rickety balconies lived my family - a mother who didn't want me. "What will I say in person?"

Michael opened his door and came around to open mine. "How about we go in, knock on the door and see who answers? Your mother probably doesn't live here anymore. The address is at least fifteen years old." He reached for my hand and squeezed it. "I'll be right here with you." He slipped on his sunglasses to hide his bright blue eyes and appear less obvious.

It seemed pointless to me. With my luck, we were probably walking into a den of Grollics. Glasses or no glasses, they would know what he was instantly. I knew I needed to stop assuming the worst. He was probably right after all. In a place like this, it was unlikely that she still lived there.

I forced a smile, trying to absorb his courage and lack of fear. "Alright. Let's go see what's behind curtain number three." I was nervous but something else ran alongside the anxiety... hope. I didn't want to have any, but I did; and I knew I'd be disappointed if the address led us to a dead end.

We walked, hand-in-hand, to the building's entrance. A tall, overweight man sat on a concrete bench wearing a stained undershirt and old, worn pants. He stared blankly at us, not even bothering to hide the large can he held in his hand. It was a very generic brand of beer, only marked BEER in green against a yellow background. From the smell of him, it was obvious that it wasn't his first of the day. This man matched the surroundings, blending in with the decay and filth everywhere. The jeep, our clothes, and basic cleanliness were something completely out of the norm here. I moved closer to Michael, not even realizing I'd done so until I bumped against him and had to catch myself from stumbling. "Sorry," I mumbled.

A low chuckle escaped his lips. "That guy's harmless. Big, but not a Grollic. No mark. Just a really bad aroma."

"I didn't even think to check for it." I hit the heel of my hand against my forehead. "I was too busy trying to figure out his brand of beer."

He ignored my lame joke, didn't even crack a smile. "If it's there for the seeing, you always need to look." Michael opened the dirty glass door for me. After letting me in first to the small entrance, he lifted his glasses to check the names on the intercom system. "I don't see her name. I bet the numbers don't correspond to the actual apartment numbers. It looks like it had been done alphabetically at one point a long time ago, but loads of names have been added. Who knows which one's even a legit name?"

As he continued staring at the list, I tried the door to the lobby. It opened. "Lock's broke."

Michael turned and shrugged. "Yeah, guess we could have tried that first."

"If it's there for the seeing, you always need to look." I laughed at his silly grin. "Seems we make a good team."

"Never doubted that for a moment."

We headed inside and paused at the out of order elevators. The sign looked as ancient as the intercom system. Michael opened the door to the stairs, stepping in first this time. "Let me go first. I don't trust closed in spaces." He led the way to the third floor. No one entered the stuffy stairwell.

It took a moment to find the correct apartment door, the last number was missing off the door.

I inhaled a deep breath through my nose and let it out slowly through my mouth. "Here's goes." I knocked quietly and then rapped hard twice. I felt Michael tense beside me. He probably heard movement inside before my human ears could. Sure enough, a moment later a chain lock slid on the other side of the door, followed by another. I swallowed nervously.

The knob turned. "Marcus, wha—" the voice stopped short when the door opened fully. A boy about my age, maybe a year or two older, stood staring at me, mouth open. It was difficult to tell his exact age, the hard look on his face showed years of experience that had nothing to do with numbers. He glanced at Michael and took a step back. "What the hell?" His gaze flitted back to me.

He was definitely a few years older. He was as tall as Michael, but dark hair and complexion. I couldn't stop staring at his eyes. They were nearly the same color as mine. "Who are you?" I blurted unable to stop myself.

His gaze narrowed as he glanced once more at Michael quickly and then back to me. He set his hands on his hips, his biceps bulging. "Who the hell are you?"

Michael stepped in front of me, his foot halfway through the door. "Where looking for somebody. Is your mother around?"

The boy scoffed. He was obviously too old to still be living with his mom. "My mother? She's having a rest. You can go find her down the road."

My heart rate sped up. He might be my brother. His eyes sure seemed to say we were related. I might have a brother? The thought had never occurred to me. I might have a brother!

"Could you be a little more specific?" Michael enunciated each syllable crisply.

"At Saint Andrews."

She was at a church? My mind was apparently frozen with stupid ice.

"Thanks." Michael turned to go steering me by the elbow so I walked in front of him.

"You aren't going to get much from her." The boy called down the hall.

I swung around, part of me wanting to see him one more time so I could burn the image of his face in my mind. I peered around Michael. "Why's that?"

"She's at Saint Andrew's cemetery. She's been there the better part of ten years."

My stomach dropped. "You're mother was Rebekah Gnowee?" *Please say no, please say no.*

He nodded. His eyes sympathetic a moment before they turned hard and unreadable again. His head tilted to the side, his brows furrowed together. "Jamie?"

I shook my head. "My name's Rouge."

Michael beat me to my next question. "Who are you?"

"Robert. Why are you looking for my mother?" He didn't bother hiding the suspicion in his voice. It came out more as an accusation then a question.

"It doesn't matter anymore." Michael who had been standing quietly behind me reached for my hand. "We need to go," he whispered curtly.

Robert crossed his arms over his muscular chest. "You shouldn't be here, Jamie – Rouge – whatever your name is. Especially with HIM." He glared at Michael.

I imagined the hair on the back of Robert's neck rising. The obvious dawned on me a second too late. "Crap!" Robert was a Grollic. Michael obviously had realized a lot sooner. "We're leaving. Sorry to have bothered you." I started backing away, my eyes trained on his neck imagining his birthmark just below his collar bone.

The stairwell door swung open with a loud bang. I jumped and Michael crouched ready to pounce. A burly guy about the same age as Robert bounded into the hall. Assessing the situation, his eyes burned from brown to a light color.

Yellow.

He was a bloody Grollic.

"What do we have here?"

"A mistake." Michael's voice stayed even and smooth.

I envied his ability to stay so calm.

"My apologies." Michael took my hand, pulling me to his other side so he stood between the stranger and me.

The guy spent way too much time in the gym. He was huge. If he turned into a Grollic, I had no idea what kind of chance Michael and I stood between him and Rob. What if I couldn't control them? Sweat began to form as small beads on my forehead.

"Rob?" Big guy glanced down behind us where Rob now stood only a few feet away. "Do these guys need to be escorted out the building?"

Rob grinned. It looked more like a snarl of sarcasm. "Be my guest."

"We're fine." Michael's always composed features were beginning to crumble. "We know the way out."

"I'm sure you do." The stranger stepped to the side to let us through the stairwell. "This isn't the best neighborhood. I saw your Jeep outside. Might be better if I walk with you."

Michael held his gaze, even and hard. "Fine. How about we get this fine young lady to the Jeep, then you and I have a nice chat?"

The guy burst out laughing. "I'll be up shortly, Rob." Marcus waved-off his friend like he couldn't care less.

We started down the stairs, Michael making sure I was in front, then him and then the Grollic.

"Dude, I have no idea who the hell you are, but you have a serious set a cahones's on you. Why the hell would you bring a sheep into the lion's den?"

Michael didn't stop walking down the stairs, he kept close to me. "I didn't know. We were trying to find someone. It doesn't matter... obviously a dead end."

They arrived in the lobby. I had no idea how my legs carried me across to the door that led outside.

As we passed the big, fat guy on the bench, he suddenly came to life. "Marcus! Marcus Brutus! How is your mama? I 'aven't seen her in ages!" The man stood and hugged burly Marcus.

"Go!" Michael hissed, pushing me into a run.

I raced to the car, the door already open and the end running before I even reached it. Michael pulled into gear and tore away from the curb, tires squealing, dirt and debris flying behind us.

Chapter 13

'Holy guacamole!– I shouted, whipping around to see if Marcus had turned into a Grollic and was chasing us down.

Two figures stood, one with his hands on his head, the other with his hands in the air. They grew smaller and smaller as Michael pressed on the gas pedal. He kept checking the rearview mirror and every window for a blind spot, obviously expecting a Grollic to come out behind some building or house and ram itself into the Jeep.

He took a hard right and shifted gears. 'What did you just say?– he asked a few minutes later, finally slowing downing down slightly and rolling through a stop sign.

'I didn't say anything.– I glanced all around me again, my heart refusing to slow its frantic pace.

'I believe you did.– He chuckled. 'I think you said *holy guacamole*?–

My eyes rolled toward the roof of the Jeep. 'I might have.– I punched him lightly in the arm. 'It was an intense moment. I wasn't thinking straight.–

'You've got quite the foul mouth on you!– He smiled and winked at me, then veered the Jeep toward the I90 and took the on ramp to the interstate. 'I'm just going to drive around a bit. Make sure we aren't being followed.–

'Sounds good to me. You can just keep driving back to Port Q if you want. You won't get any arguments from me.–

' Till we're halfway home. Then you're going to want to come back and find out what the heck just happened.–

' No. I think I'm completely fine with never having to go there again. I have the file…–I glanced down on the ground by my feet. ' I can start " where is the file?–I shifted and checked to see if I was sitting on it. I felt under the seat and unclicked my seatbelt to check the back. ' It's not here!–Panic found its way back into my chest. ' Michael, stop the car! Where's the file?–

He made his way over to the right lane and pulled off on the next exit. At the same time he checked his seat and around him. He drove into a Walmart parking lot and jumped out of the Jeep to get a better look.

I did the same. The file wasn't there. A shaky sigh escaped my mouth, and I could feel my lower lip begin to tremble. I hated crying. Fighting the tears, my throat tightened and throbbed. I couldn't believe the file was gone. I'd just had it in my hands, had read so little of it, and now it was gone. What a day! What a freakin"awful day!

Michael came around the Jeep and pulled me into his arms.

I pressed my face hard into his chest, still trying to fight the tears that refused to stop. ' It's gone,–I mumbled over and over again.

He ran his fingers lightly over my scalp and hair. ' Shhh…–he said as he tried to comfort me. ' It must have fallen out when we took off.–

We stayed together, arms wrapped around each other for a long time. Finally I straightened and tucked a lock of messy hair behind my ear. ' I have a name. It's a start.–

' It is.–He wiped a tear from my cheek. ' And it appears you might have a brother.–

' Bit of an asshole, isn't he?–

Michael eyes went big before he burst out laughing. ' Your foul mouth is progressing today.–

' Hey, if the word fits...–I smiled but it quickly faded. ' He called me Jamie. Maybe he thinks I'm someone else. The name on my birth information that was in the f-file says my mother named me Rouge.–I shook my head. ' I don't get it.–

' He probably doesn't know who you are.–

' Yeah... Well, he did know what you were though. He's a wolf, so is that Marcus Brutus.–I sighed. ' I wasn't expecting things to be peachy and pretty, but I didn't expect this.–

Michael put his arm around me. I savored the warmth he offered and rested my head against his shoulder. ' Maybe we should just go home. Pack our stuff up. Let sleeping dogs lie.–

He kissed the top of my head. His hot breath sent a shiver down my spine, the good kind. ' Let's head back to the hotel and decide from there.–

' Okay.–I let him help me back into the Jeep, and we drove in silence back to the Holiday Inn.

In our room, I pulled out the Wolf Book and the journal I'd been writing in. I sat on the bed, my back against the headboard and stared at the ancient leather book. Tapping my foot against the sheets, I straightened up and grabbed my pen. I planned to write what had happened down in my journal, then turn the page and never think of it again.

Except I knew I would never forget it. I knew, whether I was afraid of the knowledge or not, there would be no guarantee I'd have the chance to learn more later. I was furious with myself. I should have taken the time to read the full file before running off on any leads. Stupid, stupid mistake! Why had I been so rash in my decision making? I stole a glance at Michael.

He sat behind his laptop at the desk. We worked quietly, completely comfortable in each other's silence. He had no idea of the inner turmoil going on inside of me.

He stood just as I was closing my journal. ' Do you feel like going out to eat?–

I shook my head.

'Why don't I go grab some take out then? What do you feel like?–

I shrugged. I felt drained. Disappointed in myself. Tired. 'I'm fine with anything. I'll just chill till you get back.– I pointed to his laptop. ' Do you mind if I look a few things up?–

' Go for it.–He grabbed the keys and his wallet. ' I'll be quick.–

I jumped up and ran over to him. My weird history and somehow Grollic related family wasn't his fault. He didn't care, maybe I shouldn't either so much. ' I love you.– I arched onto my toes and pressed my lips against his. 'Very much.– I kissed him again.

His hands cupped my jawline and his fingers pressed against my neck just under my ears. His mouth opened to deep the kiss, his tongue slipping into my mouth.

My hands curled into fist of pleasure against his chest grabbing his shirt and gently tugging at it.

He smiled against my lips and whispered, his breath hot against my skin. ' I'm only going for dinner. I'll be back in less than twenty minutes.–

' I know.–I refused to let go of him.

' Or I could just stay here.– He laughed when my stomach rumbled. ' Duty calls.–He stepped back and saluted me. ' I need to feed my lady.– He stole a kiss before opening the door and disappearing behind it.

I stood, my fingers pressed against my lips, enjoying the bliss I felt whenever we kissed.

Finally I moved to the desk and sat down. I opened up Internet Explorer and googled Gnowee.

I grabbed my journal and jotted down a summary of the word. It was based on mythology of the Aboriginals of south-eastern Australia. Gnowee was a solar goddess whose torch was the Sun. I skimmed over most of that part of the information, just writing down: Gnowee = Solar Goddess.

Reading more, I added other notes. Gnowee was once a woman who lived on the earth at a time when it was eternally dark. One day she left her little child sleeping while she went out to dig for yams. Food was scarce, and Gnowee wandered so far that she reached the end of the earth, passed under it and emerged on the other side. Not knowing where she was, she could not find her little child anywhere, so she climbed into the sky with her great torch to get a clearer view. She still wanders the sky to this day, lighting the whole world with her torch as she continues to search for her lost child.

Some of the stories said the child was a son, other"s didn"t mention a gender.

I liked the story. I didn"t know why, but I did. It made me feel like maybe my mother was looking for me. I"m sure every kid whose parents left them felt like this.

I added some personal thoughts into my journal after I wrote the story down.

Note to Self:

The story could represent my mother. Like some mythology tale that represented something in the far distant future. Maybe my mother never wanted to give me up. Or maybe the life here was not what she wanted for me. Or because I didn't bear the mark on below my collar bone, she couldn't bear to bring me up.

I believe I have a brother who doesn't know I exist. My mother is gone. Did she die? Was she murdered? What happened? What of a father? I always wanted to find the woman who gave me up but never considered a father. What if he wanted me and my mother did not?

These are questions I am never going to find the answers to.

Michael returned with two large carry out bags. He set them out on the dresser. Appetizers, pasta, wings, pizza, chicken fingers, and four different kinds of desserts filled the make-shift counter. ' I wasn"t sure what you wanted, so I picked up a bunch of stuff.–

I put my journal and the Wolf Book into my back pack and grabbed a plate. ' It smells awesome!–

He turned the television on to a movie and settled down beside me on the bed. ' If you spill, that"s your side,–he teased.

' Or I can just roll on top of you.–I winked slyly.

The slice of pizza in his hand slipped out, landing on the bed.

I burst out laughing. ' That"s your side!–I ate some of everything and then tried the desserts. I had been starving, but now felt ready to burst. I changed in the bathroom into comfy shorts and a top, and crawled under the sheets beside Michael, snuggling close against him.

My eyes grew drowsy as I fought to stay awake. We had a hotel room, alone, all to ourselves, and I couldn"t stop myself from napping? I yawned. Some amazing girlfriend I was!

Sleep won in the end, and I let myself succumb to it. I decided I"d make up for it the next night.

Chapter 14

Michael called my name softly, "Rouge? Sweetie, do you want some coffee?'

I rolled over and rubbed my face. "Did you make it?' I grimaced and then opened my eyes a slit. I stared vacantly at him, trying to remember where I was. It took a moment, but the memory of the previous day came flooding back eventually.

"I went to Starbucks.'

I sat up and yawned, then inhaled deeply into the cup he offered. "Hmmm... smells good.'

"You okay?'

I took a small sip, enjoyed the latte foam on the top that seemed to clear away some of the cobwebs in my mouth. "I'm okay.' I glanced over at the alarm clock by the side of the bed. Eleven thirty. "You went out now for coffee? It's so late!' The thick curtain covered the window blocking out the street lights.

"It's eleven thirty A-M.' He smiled, his eyes sparkling. "You were dead to the world. I figured coffee was my only option.'

"It's morning?!' So much for the romantic, virgin-taking evening I had planned.

"Almost lunch.' Michael pulled the curtain away from the window and the shade cover to let the sun in. "Is there anything you want to do today?'

I sipped my coffee and stared blankly in front of me. I'd dreamt about my invisible mother flying through the sky with a bark torch lighting her way. I knew what I wanted to do... getting Michael to let me do it was another question. "I want to go to Saint Andrew's Cemetery.'

Michael blinked several times but kept his face unreadable. "No.'

I ignored his reply. "Then I want to find out how she died.'

"No.'

I set the latte down and stood. "I'm not going to let two Grollics stop me. You said yourself yesterday that we came here to find answers. I'm going to find them.'

"Yesterday you wanted to go home.' He began to pace, reminding me of Caleb.

"Today, I want answers.' I put my hands on my hips. "And I want my file back.'

"We should check with Caleb, maybe get some back up. Or plan this out better. Yesterday was my fault. I was stupid not to think through everything that could happen.'

The thought of Caleb stepping in to help annoyed me. "I don't want Caleb here. This is my fight.'

"It isn't a fight, Rouge,' Michael said quietly.

"Like hell it isn't! This is *my* fight!' I grabbed clothes out of the suitcase. "I'm going to shower and go. You can stay here or you can come with me. I don't care.' I did care, I just couldn't admit it out loud. I wanted Michael with me, not Caleb with his condescending stare and annoyingly insightful, guilt-inducing comments.

Michael watched me stomp to the bathroom. I could feel his eyes on me. When I slammed the door and locked it, I heard him mutter to himself, "What's gotten into her?'

I showered and changed in less than ten minutes. While in the shower I tried to figure out how I woke with such a feeling of dead calm; not the kind of calm that comes with peace and acceptance, the kind where you know trouble is lurking just around the corner, and there's nothing stopping you from running head-long into it; the kind of feeling that made you want to run towards the trouble instead of away from it, to get resolutions from it. I had no clue where it came from, but I had no intention of letting it pass me by. It would get answers. Without fear. Without feeling or sentiment. I needed them, now.

"Ready to go?' I asked as I stepped out of the bathroom and grabbed my backpack. I'd dressed in capri pants and a black shirt, and felt a little like Lara Croft. I wanted easy movement in case I had to make a run for it at some point today.

"Sure.' Michael gave me a strange look but didn't say anything else.

We took the elevator in silence.

Outside I walked to the passenger side of the Jeep and waited for Michael to unlock the doors. He hit the button on the keys and went to the back, pulling open the rear door. I came around, wedged between the jeeps door and the board on board fence of the property line.

Michael pulled a suitcase I hadn't noticed toward him and opened it. Inside lay strange weapons and knives. He handed me a knife with a cover on the blade, and also another weapon that looked like a gun. "It's a like a tazor. You're not shooting bullets but it will freeze or throw a Grollic off for a few seconds.'

I tossed it in my backpack and went around while he fiddled around with items for himself. "You do remember we're going to a cemetery, right?'

He grunted in reply, finally slammed the back door shut and then came around to the driver's side. "They might not be on to you, but they are on to me. I don't feel like dying today if it can be avoided.' He leaned over and touched the pendant around my neck. "Keep that safe with you always.'

We drove back toward the less than privileged end of town, avoiding the road with the apartment on it.

"Are you sure you want to do this?' Michael asked as the cemetery came into view.

I nodded. "I don't see anyone here.' No Grollics was my unspoken comment.

Michael pulled the Jeep to the curb and stopped in front of the cathedral church. "I want you to wait here. Let me check the cemetery first.'

"No one's here,' I repeated.

"I know!' His voice rose in frustration. "There look to be over three hundred stones, angels, raised and flat monuments. It'll be quicker if you let me run through and look. We could be here for two days looking otherwise.' He picked his perfectly clean fingernail. "And it doesn't hurt to double check.'

I opened my mouth to protest but he cut me off before I had a chance.

"Give me ten minutes. I promise I'll be back by then.' He checked the review and stepped out of the Jeep. "Wait in the driver's seat... just in case.' He leaned in again. "And lock the doors!'

Low blow. Damon had gotten into the Jeep because I hadn't locked it. Michael didn't seem to have a problem subtlety reminding me.

I obeyed and crawled over the stick shift into the driver" seat. I blew a kiss to his back as he sped off. I set my watch and watched it count up to two minutes, then glanced at the graves to see if I could find Michael or any eminent danger.

Nothing.

Until I glanced to my right and nearly screamed out load.

Marcus Brutus sat on the stairs leading up to the church. He waved when I noticed him.

My fingers reached for the knife on my belt as I looked around the entire vehicle for a hidden Grollic just waiting to pounce.

He stood and sauntered over to me, motioning me to roll down the window.

Grabbing my purse I hid the knife in there close by the tazer, ready to grab either one if I needed it.

I let the window down a crack.

Marcus watched it and then shrugged. "I'm not here to fight.' He held his hands up in surrender.

"What do you want?' My eyes darted toward the tombs, trying to see if Michael was visible or if any beasts might be chasing him down.

"Nobody's there. Just your buddy.' He reached around him as I squeezed the tazer inside my purse, ready to use it.

Marcus pulled out a manila envelope his back. A loud sigh of relief escaped through my lips. I had thought he was going to draw a gun.

"I believe this is yours.' He slid it through the slightly opened window.

I realized it was the file folder. "What are you giving this back to me?'

Marcus shrugged. "It belongs to you.'

"Aren't you going to piss a few Grollics off... you being here?'

"Very much. We're all sworn to protect this area and never let you back in it.'

What did he just say? "Back in?'

He nodded, checking for Michael before looking back at her. "I shouldn't be here. This is a mistake.' He started to back away.

"No!' I jumped out of the Jeep and ran around it. "You need to tell me what's going on. Please!'

He hesitated. "Look,' he said, shooting a glance toward the cemetery. "I know who you are and I'm torn between helping you or protecting my ass and my pack.'

"What do you mean?' I heard Michael call me name.

Marcus flinched, his eyes burning to a yellow color. "Meet me back here at dusk. Alone. I trust you but I...' he began running in the opposite direction that Michael had taken. "I don't trust the dead-walker,' he shouted before tearing around the street corner.

I stared at the spot he had turned and I'd lost view of him because of the church building.

"Rouge, why are you out of the Jeep?' Michael touched my shoulder.

I jumped, unaware he had returned. "I... I thought I heard you call my name.'

He shook his head. "I found your mother's stone. It's safe. Nobody's here.' He held his hand out to me.

I entwined my fingers with his and let him lead me through the old and new gravestones. My heart was torn; should I tell him about Marcus, or forget the Grollic had found me, or did I go and meet him tonight? He could be planning to ambush me. Or he could be trying to help and just not sure if the risk was worth losing everything if he did.

I sighed. I wished I could ask Michael, but I knew he would never let me come here on my own. And Marcus would never believe me if I told him Michael was safe. Trust had to be earned. No werewolf would even consider trusting a "dead-walker' as Marcus had called them. I thought back to Damon. He had been big and burly like Marcus, but different.

"Harder to do this then you thought?' Michael squeezed my hand. "You never knew the woman and yet you feel connected to her.'

I nodded, guilt washing over me for letting Michael believe it was for something else.

"We're almost there.' He pointed, using our hands together to show where the stone was. "It's very clean. Someone's been taking care of her stone.'

We walked along a row of raised and flat stones. Michael stopped me in front of a raised soft gray marble stone. I nearly laughed aloud. On top sat a small angel similar to the one I had nearly decapitated the day I met Michael. The only difference was this angel had her wings spread, as if looking down on the stone.

Rebekah Gnowee
Here for but a moment.

I ran my finger over the engraved letters. The stone had been there for over ten years but looked new. A bouquet of flowers lay near the base in a vase screwed into the marble. "Someone misses her.' I kneeled on the grass before the stone wishing I had brought flowers as well. "I wonder how she died?' I said the thought out loud.

"When we get back to the hotel, I'll call Caleb and see if he can find some medical records or a copy of the death certificate. We have a name and an address, it shouldn't be too hard to find.'

I remembered Marcus" words and wondered what he knew about Rebekah Gnowee. He could have information that a death certificate or any medical records would never show. I realized I didn't have a choice. I had to see him that night.

Chapter 15

I wrote in my journal and waited for time to pass after we returned to the hotel. Michael tried calling Caleb, which went straight to voicemail. He left Caleb a message to call him back when he had a chance. I spent the time trying to figure out how I would get out without Michael. It was going to be impossible.

"What do you want to do for dinner tonight?" he asked just as his phone rang. He glanced down. "It's Caleb."

The perfect moment had just landed in my lap. "You talk to him and I'll go grab us some dinner." I grabbed the keys and my purse, slipping the wolf book under it so he wouldn't see. "I'll surprise you with something local that's really good." I didn't give him a chance to reply. I kissed his cheek. "Answer the phone, silly. You know how Caleb is." I winked and forced myself to walk a normal pace out the door without looking back.

In the hall I broke into a run, taking the stairs to save time. Outside I walked to the Jeep and glanced at our hotel room window. Michael stood by the window, phone to his ear. I waved and smiled before unlocking the Jeep and pulling out of the parking lot.

I took the same route Michael had driven earlier. My hands shook against the steering wheel so I gripped it tightly to try and stop the tremors. I might be scared but Marcus was risking everything to talk to me.

The sun had started its decent. I had about twenty, maybe twenty-five minutes before Michael would start to worry and begin calling and looking for me.

I slowed the Jeep as I turned on the road just before Saint Andrews. Butterflies hammered against the inside of my stomach when I saw Marcus sitting on the steps waiting. I swallowed and pulled the Jeep to the curb. It took several deep breaths to physically calm myself. I grabbed my bag and slipped it over my shoulder, only pausing to stuff the Wolf Book inside. I had no idea why I brought it, except I was somehow, magically, hoping to draw strength from it.

He was alone. At least nobody seemed to be hiding behind a bush or in the cemetery. I tried to make my face unreadable as I walked over and sat down beside him. I planned to stay in plain sight and if the need to protect myself arose, I had the taser Michael had given me in my bag, the knife on my belt, and the words of the Wolf Book in my head. I figured I could manage.

"You came." Marcus smirked. "I, uh, wasn't sure you would."

"I did. Now what did you want to tell me?" I was hesitant to be his buddy.

He chuffed. "You've no idea, do you?"

I had somewhat of an idea. I just wasn't going to tell him.

"How old are you? Seventeen?"

He obviously didn't know as much as he thought he did. "About that."

"When did you get your file?"

"Yesterday."

"Oh... so you just found out about Rebekah?" He reached for my knee but dropped his hand before touching me.

"Yeah."

Marcus rocked his feet back and forth. He sighed, his big chest rising and dropping. "She was good. There's not a lot of good in this group here."

"Group of Grollics?"

He gave me a funny look. "Of course. What you think we are? A bunch of half breeds?"

"You can mix?" By the annoyed look on his face, I'd hit a nerve. "I... I don't know much about werewo-Grollics."

"You seriously don't know anything?"

I played with my keys for a moment, debating what I should reveal. In the end, I didn't know much anyway and saw no point in trying to hide that. "I know about the birthmark below you collar bone and you can shift. Michael's different."

"Yeah, he's the enemy."

"He's not. If you—"

"He's part of the Higher Coven. Or somewhere close to it. It's obvious by the way he walks and holds himself. I can't imagine he let you come here alone." He glanced up the road. "Is he hiding somewhere or got you on a mike?"

"No." I sighed and watched the setting sun. "He thinks I'm grabbing dinner."

"Good."

"Good?"

Marcus stood. "Let's take a walk."

"No. I'm more comfortable staying here." I reached inside my bag, my fingers touching the taser.

"I just figured we could walk through the cemetery as we talk." He remained standing, waiting for me to get up and follow him, which I had no intention of doing. He eventually figured that out "Fine. What do you want to know?"

The question threw me. He had been the one so adamant about helping me and now he seemed annoyed that I wanted information. It didn't make sense. "Why did Rob say I shouldn't be here?"

"Because you shouldn't. We're controlled by a...an alpha." He tilted his head. "Does that make sense?" When I nodded, he continued. "We're not allowed to let you here. If you show up, you're supposed to be toast." He made a line with his hand across his neck.

"Then why aren't you doing the same? If you're controlled by the alpha?" I stood, slipping my purse over my shoulder. Suddenly my gut was telling me I needed to leave soon.

"I am."

"You're what?"

"Controlled by the alpha."

"Rebekah wasn't." I had no idea how I knew that, but I just did.

He spat. "That's because she wasn't a Grollic."

My eyebrows pushed together. I opened my mouth but nothing came out.

"She stuck around because of Rob." He snorted. "Took the beatings. All of it."

Someone beat Rebekah?

"Rob's going to come after you. He wants you dead." He gave me the once over. "Maybe Rebekah stuck around because she was waiting for you."

"I doubt it." I checked my watch. I didn't like where this conversation was going. "Look. I need to get going. Michael's going to start worrying. We're leaving. I promise we won't come back. I won't tick off your alpha anymore." I started for the Jeep.

Marcus' hand came up and blocked my chest. "You're not going anywhere."

I pushed his arm away. "Don't." I reached in my purse and pulled out the taser-thing.

He laughed and kicked it out of my hand before I could even find the on-switch. It flew in the air in a perfect arc and landed down the sidewalk, shattering into about fifty pieces.

I shook my hand, pretty sure he'd broken a finger.

"You don't stand a chance against me. As a Grollic or human." He snarled and then shoved me down against the stairs. Flexing his large biceps, he pulled a gun out from behind him, jamming the barrel against my forehead. "Get up and walk!"

Panic thrashed through me. In snippets, I tried to think of what
to say to stop him. If I managed to speak in the language to control
the Grollics, would it work on him in human form? My legs
shaking, I still found the courage to stand. Terror hadn't frozen me
to the spot, although it should have. I realized my mistake now. I
should never have trusted a Grollic. In my experience, they were all
terrible monsters. Not one was worth saving. Anger burned inside. I
clenched my fists and started marching in the direction he pointed
– toward the cemetery. I knew I wasn't invincible; that a gun would
kill me, but at that point, I was hoping for options to show up as I
went. Staying still or resisting would only get me killed faster.

He stayed close to me, the gun pressing into my back, right
behind my heart. "Stop!" he barked when we reached Rebekah's
gravestone.

I froze. The anger I had felt just a moment before had liquefied
to fear as we walked through the rows of marble stones. I needed
the anger back. It was the only way I could try to control him the
way the wolf book had taught me.

Marcus' hand squeezed my shoulder. He shoved me down to my
knees.

The barrel of the gun now pressed against the base of my skull.

I shut my eyes tight. "Please d—"

The gun flew away from my temple as Marcus stumbled away
from me. He rolled on the ground and crouched, ready to pounce.

"Stay away from her!" A voice hissed.

My head swiveled toward the sound. Not Michael. I turned
around, still on my knees.

Robert.

A very angry looking, yellow eyed Robert.

Marcus laughed. "Buddy!" He straightened. "I was wondering
when you would get here. You want to finish it yourself?"

"What're you doing, Marcus?" Robert glared at him. "I
thought—"

"You thought wrong." Marcus took a step forward, his body rigid with anger. He jabbed a finger at me. "That bitch needs to die. She'll destroy all of us."

"I'm your acting Alpha and I'm telling you to stand down." Robert's eyes never left Marcus.

"And I'm telling you, you're wrong. Think of the law." Marcus studied Robert's eyes, chest heaving, as if he was waiting for some change. When he realized that Robert wasn't going to change his view, he charged.

The sound of bone impacting bone made me cringe. They wrestled back and forth in front of me, blood flowing freely from punches and flinging into the air, to land on the gravestones around me. I wedged myself tight against Rebekah's stone, trying to understand what was going on. Robert was fighting for me? Why?

"I'll kill you too." Marcus had gained ground, and had managed to throw Robert to the ground. The back of his head hit an upraised stone, breaking a piece of it off. His eyes went out of focus, switching from yellow back to hazel. He was still alive, but dazed.

Marcus grabbed the chunk of marble and held it high over his head. "You're just like *her*. Weak."

Robert gritted his teeth, filling up with some kind of energy that came out of nowhere, his eyes burning like fire. "My mother was never weak!" He threw Marcus off of him and attacked, his body starting to shift into wolf form.

Marcus rolled out of the way and began shifting as well.

"Don't change!" I shouted my hands pushing straight out in front of me, trying to will them to stop.

They both froze and looked at me with bewildered animal eyes – like a deer in headlights.

Marcus recovered faster than Robert, racing toward him like a football player ready to tackle his opponent. Robert reached for something on the ground by him and held it close to him as Marcus jumped.

I jerked and covered my ears as the gunshot echoed in the nearly silent cemetery.

Red wetness began to cover Marcus' back. He rolled off of Robert, clutching his chest. "W-Why?" His eyes faded back to their human blue. "I'm your pack, your brother."

"We are brothers." Robert got up, gun still trained on Marcus. He moved close to me, protectively standing in front. He fired the gun again and Marcus's head fell back, his eyes staring vacantly up at the sky. "But you're not my blood."

Chapter 16

I stared at Robert, unable or unwilling to comprehend what he had just done. It sunk in slowly. "You killed him."

"I know." Robert slipped the gun into the back of his jeans. "He was going to kill you... and me as well."

"Why? He said he wanted to help me."

Robert gave me a strange look. "He lied."

"What do we do now?"

"I don't know about you, but I have to leave."

"I mean, about the body?"

"Leave it. The others will be here soon and can deal with it." He turned to go, paused and turned around. "I just saved you. Can you turn off that voo-doo spell you shouted that stopped me from shifting?"

"Pardon?" I felt like I'd been hit on the head.

"You spoke some weird command or something. I can't shift now. If I've gotta run, I need to protect myself."

"I don't know what I did." Then I remembered, I'd yelled at them to stop. I leaned back against my mother's stone for support. I'd done it again. Spoken Grollic.

"Can you hurry it up?"

"I don't know to take it off."

Robert began to pace. "You're joking! I just broke the one law we were commanded to follow! I'm so fucked!"

"I'll figure it out. Give me a sec." I tried to think of something to undo the words. "Forget what I said," I tried.

"Forget what? You didn't say anything." Robert stopped pacing and waited.

"Was that in English?"

"Yeah." He grabbed me by my elbow and began moving out of the cemetery, toward the Jeep. "You don't know how to use it, do you?" He lowered his voice, "Keep walking, fast."

A car drove past and parked near the other end of the cemetery.

"I kinda only just figured out I could do it." I held my purse tight, feeling the need to protect the Wolf Book inside. "Are you my brother?"

He nodded curtly. "I'm the sixth. You're the seventh."

"Oh." I had no idea what that meant, but at the moment it seemed better to leave than the try to figure it out.

"Rouge!" Michael's shout brought me out of my stupor.

I pushed past Robert and ran toward the sound. Michael stood by the Jeep, his face etched in worry. "You okay?" He scowled at Robert.

"How did you know where to find me?"

"There's a tracker on the Jeep. When you didn't come back, I checked it." He opened the passenger door. "Get inside."

"Wait." I knew what he planned to do. "Rob saved me. He just killed Marcus."

Michael hesitated a moment. Then looked to Robert for confirmation.

"Yeah." Robert walked up and stopped in front of me, his hands crossing over his chest. "Now can you fix me?"

Michael and Robert glanced toward the cemetery at the same time.

"Get in," Michael commanded. He pulled the passenger seat forward and I crawled into the back. "You, too," he said to Robert before racing around to the driver's side.

Robert complied. Michael revved the engine and did a fast U-turn. We drove in silence as he raced away from the church.

"You can drop me off here." Robert tapped the window.

"No." Michael focused on the road in front of him. "You've just given yourself a death wish by choosing Rouge over your pack."

"I know." Robert glanced back at me. "Can you fix me now?"

"What are you talking about?" Michael asked.

"I somehow commanded Robert and Marcus to stop shifting."

Michael smirked. "You did the wolf-thing again?"

"Apparently."

He glanced in the review mirror and winked at me, then his face turned serious. "Looks like you're coming with us, Rob."

"Excuse me?"

"You can't stay here. They'll kill you." Michael ignored the and-you-won't questioning look Rob gave him. "You can't shift so you're vulnerable. Until Rouge can change you back, you need protection. I owe you that for saving her."

Rob scowled at us. "It sounds more like I'm your prisoner." At least he didn't try to argue or jump out of the fast moving Jeep.

"I hope you don't need anything from your apartment. We can't go back there."

"I don't." Rob rubbed his forehead. "We leaving for good?"

Michael nodded. "Just need to grab our stuff from the hotel." He pulled into the hotel parking lot. "I'll run in and grab it. You guys wait here." He was out of the Jeep before either of us could protest.

Rob waited till Michael disappeared through the front doors. "Are you *with* him?"

I nodded, trying and failing, to avoid seeing the disgusted look on his face. It made me angry. What right did he have to be disgusted of me and who I chose to be with? "You know you're lousy at hiding your feelings. You should work on that."

"So are you." He frowned and then grinned. "You look like mom."

"Rebekah?" Wind seemed to rush by my ears.

"Yeah, mom."

"She's not my mother." I looked out the window, wishing Michael would hurry. "She might have given birth to me, but she dumped me off and left me." I shot him a quick glance. "She obviously didn't do that to you."

"Jamie, you—"

"My name is Rouge."

He waved a hand in the air. "Whatever. You were Jamie when I knew you."

I hesitated. "You knew me?"

"I was four when you were born."

"Then why did Rebekah try to get rid me, change her mind and then change it again? Sounds pretty flighty to me."

"She had to."

Michael came out of the hotel with our stuff, stopping me from asking Robert why. Michael tossed the suitcases, my backpack and his laptop in the back of the Jeep. He slammed the back door and then jumped into the driver's seat. "All set. Anywhere else we need to stop?"

Rob spoke up, "In Grand Island, I've got something I need to pick up."

A thought occurred to me. "Have you had to run before?"

"A few times." Robert shrugged. "But I've always come back." He paused a moment, staring out the window with a sadness I didn't understand at the time. "This time....well, I can't now. Not ever."

Michael paid the toll over the Grand Island Bridge, but he didn't miss a beat in the conversation. "Why'd you have to run? You're the Alpha of this pack here, aren't you?"

"I was," Robert corrected. "But I did have to run. My mother refused, but after she died, I left whenever he came back." He glanced at me. "Always looking for you. He had the whole pack compelled to get you if you ever showed up. He preferred you alive, but dead would suffice as well."

"Who?" Michael and I asked at the same time.

"Bentos, of course."

Chapter 17

I gasped.

Michael nearly drove the Jeep off the road, swerving just in time, and getting a loud honk from a trucker's horn.

"Bentos?" I whispered, glancing at Michael to see if he was okay.

"Yeah," Robert sighed. "Son of a bitch is our father."

That floored me. I felt the blood drain from my face, my fingers went numb and my heart stuttered.

"What?" I'd figured he was a great grandfather or something. "How can he still be alive?"

"There's only one person who can kill him." Robert shook his head. "Don't you guys know any of this?" He pointed to the upcoming exit. "This is where I need to grab my stuff. Michael, you know about Bentos, right?"

"I know more than Rouge does." That caught me by surprise, but I tucked it away for the moment.

"Bentos killed Michael and his sister." I blurted out, receiving a dirty look from Michael in the rearview mirror. Obviously, he felt that now was not the time to spill secrets.

Robert laughed, slapping his knee. "Seriously? *You're* one of the twins? The twins?"

"Apparently so. Didn't realize we were famous among the Grollics." Michael said, waiting at the light. "Where do we go? Left? Right?"

"Right. See the Topps grocery store? There's a shop right beside it." Robert unclicked his seatbelt. "I'll be right back." He hopped out of the Jeep and jogged inside the small office. It looked like a packing or shipping company.

"Do you believe him?" Michael asked me quietly.

I rested my hand on his shoulder. He covered it with his own. "I do," I said.

"I don't trust him completely, but... I do too." He straightened when Robert came out of the store. "He's going to be able to answer a lot of questions you have."

"Do you believe Bentos is still alive?" I couldn't bring myself to ask what he thought of Bentos possibly being my father.

"I do. For years I wanted to kill him myself. He disappeared about fifteen years ago; just up and vanished. Now I'm starting to wonder if it was because of you."

Robert opened the door, tossed a knapsack on the seat beside me and clicked himself in. "Let's go. Tony, in the shop, said the pack is looking for me. We need to get out of here."

Michael pulled into a parking spot.

"I said—"

Michael turned on him, his eyes starting to glow blue. The mood in the Jeep reached all new levels of tenseness. "I know what you said, but get this; I'm not your pack. You're not my leader. You don't boss me around. You're in this vehicle because you saved Rouge, because she wants you here. The moment she says otherwise, you're gone."

"Robert nodded his understanding, his face set in stone, eyes fixed on Michael's but not glowing Grollic yellow. Not yet. "Trust is earned. It's a two way street. I'm not here for you. If I had the choice, you'd be lying beside Marcus. You're here because of Rouge."

"Can we just get out of this hell hole?" I interrupted them. The last thing we needed was a male showdown in the Jeep with a whole pack of Grollics on their way to rip us to shreds.

Neither spoke, but Michael pulled out of the parking space and headed back to the highway. It was quiet for a long time.

Finally, I couldn't take it anymore. "Rob, you said only one person can kill Bentos. Do you know who it is?"

He nodded. "You really don't know anything, do you?" He sighed. "I'm Bento's sixth child. It was believed that only the male's carried the Grollic gene. I don't know if evolution changed it, our environment or if it's been different all along and nobody knew, but you're Bento's daughter. His seventh child. The Seventh Mark." He pulled his shirt collar down, revealing his birthmark. It was darker than any of the others I had ever seen. "Only you can kill Bentos – and he wants you dead.

Impossible. Right? "Why?" I whispered.

"He controls the Grollics. Now you control the Grollics. Mom pretended you died in childbirth. When Bentos finally believed her, he left. She went and got you and named you Jamie. Benjamin is the name that's supposed to stop the curse from happening. Bentos means Benjamin, so Mom named you Jamie to try and stop the curse. It obviously didn't work."

"Why'd she get rid of me if she wanted to keep me?"

"Bentos came back. He would have killed you if he knew you were alive. She gave you away to protect you. When I heard about the incident on the west coast, I figured it was you." He turned in his seat, the highway lights flashing against his amber eyes, making them look yellow. "I knew you'd come back here. What I don't know is how you learned to compel the Grollics."

I reached for my purse and pulled out the Wolf Book. "I found this." I tossed it in his lap.

Robert lurched away from it, as if the leather burned him. He pushed it away. "Where the hell did you find it?"

"At a used book store."

Michael spoke, his eyes still on the dark highway in front of him. "It found its way to her. Do you know what it is?"

"I remember Bentos used to carry it around with him. He freaked and tore the town apart when he lost it. I always thought my Mom had stolen it and that was what got her killed."

I leaned over the seat and picked it up. "It's mine now."

"You know the cover's made out of Grollic skin, right?" Robert shuddered.

I didn't flinch. The fact didn't even phase me for some strange reason.

"Can you read it?" Michael asked.

"Hell, no!" Robert shook his head. "Do you know what's inside it?"

"It's Bento's journal."

"That's no journal! That's a spell book! *His* spell book. Nobody but Bentos can read it!"

"Not exactly," I said.

My eyes met Michael's in the rear view mirror.

The book slipped from my hands and fell on the seat beside me as my brain finally started to absorb all the information I'd gained in the last hour.

I had a mother who hid me to protect me? A brother I'd just compelled to stop being a Grollic? My father was alive and wanted me dead?

I was part Grollic and now a witch?

Everything had just become a lot more complicated.

~The End~

Compelled

Book 4 in the Hidden Secrets Saga - Coming
out 2015

Note from the Author;

I hope you enjoyed reading Marked By Destiny. If you have a moment to post a review to let others know about the story, I would greatly appreciate it! I love hearing from my fans so feel free to send me a message on Facebook or by email so we can chat!

All the best, W.J. May

Website: http://www.wanitamay.yolasite.com

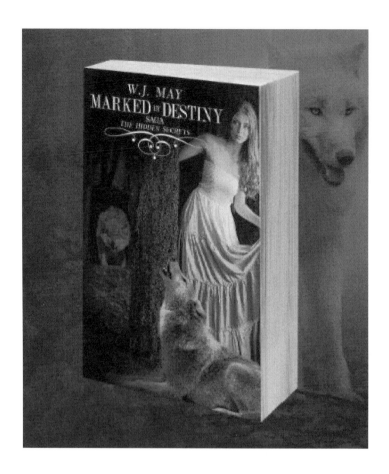

More from W.J. May

THE CHRONICLES OF KERRIGAN

Rae of Hope is FREE!

Book Trailer:

http://www.youtube.com/watch?v=gILAwXxx8MU

BOOK BLURB:

How hard do you have to shake the family tree to find the truth about the past?

Fifteen year-old Rae Kerrigan never really knew her family's history. Her mother and father died when she was young and it is only when she accepts a scholarship to the prestigious Guilder Boarding School in England that a mysterious family secret is revealed.

Will the sins of the father be the sins of the daughter?

As Rae struggles with new friends, a new school and a star-struck forbidden love, she must also face the ultimate challenge: receive a tattoo on her sixteenth birthday with specific powers that may bind her to an unspeakable darkness. It's up to Rae to undo the dark evil in her family's past and have a ray of hope for her future.

RADIUM HALOS – THE SENSELESS SERIES

Book 1 is FREE:

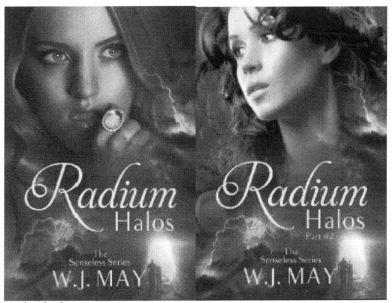

Book Blurb:

Everyone needs to be a hero at one point in their life.

The small town of Elliot Lake will never be the same again.

Caught in a sudden thunderstorm, Zoe, a high school senior from Elliot Lake, and five of her friends take shelter in an abandoned uranium mine. Over the next few days, Zoe's hearing sharpens drastically, beyond what any normal human being can detect. She tells her friends, only to learn that four others have an increased sense as well. Only Kieran, the new boy from Scotland, isn't affected.

Fashioning themselves into superheroes, the group tries to stop the strange occurrences happening in their little town. Muggings, break-ins, disappearances, and murder begin to hit too close to home. It leads the team to think someone knows about their secret – someone who wants them all dead.

An incredulous group of heroes. A traitor in the midst. Some dreams are written in blood.

Shadow of Doubt

Part 1 is FREE!
Book Trailer: http://www.youtube.com/watch?v=LZK09Fe7kgA

<u>Book Blurb:</u>

What happens when you fall for the one you are forbidden to love?

Erebus is a bit of a lost soul. He's a guy so he should be out to have fun but unlike the rest of his kind, he is solemn and withdrawn. That is, until he meets Aurora, a law student at Cornell University. His entire world is shaken. Feelings he's never had and urges he's never understood take over. These strange longings drive him to question everything about himself

When a jealous ex stalks back into his life, he must decide if he is willing to risk everything to be with Aurora. His desire for her could destroy her, or worse, erase his own existence forever.

COMING Autumn 2014:

Book Blurb:

What if courage was your only option?

When Kallie lands a college interview with the city's new hot-shot police officer, she has no idea everything in her life is about to change. The detective is young, handsome and seems to have an unnatural ability to stop the increasing local crime rate. Detective Liam's particular interest in Kallie sends her heart and head stumbling over each other.

When a raging blood feud between vampires spills into her home, Kallie gets caught in the middle. Torn between love and family loyalty she must find the courage to fight what she fears the most and possibly risk everything, even if it means dying for those she loves.

Hidden Secrets Saga:

Download Seventh Mark part 1 For FREE

Book Trailer:

http://www.youtube.com/watch?v=Y-_vVYC1gvo

ldhbfd'
B' 4'

Book Blurb:

Like most teenagers, Rouge is trying to figure out who she is and
what she wants to be. With little knowledge about her past, she has
questions but has never tried to find the answers. Everything
changes when she befriends a strangely intoxicating family. Siblings
Grace and Michael, appear to have secrets which seem connected to

Rouge. Her hunch is confirmed when a horrible incident occurs at an outdoor party. Rouge may be the only one who can find the answer.

An ancient journal, a Sioghra necklace and a special mark force life-altering decisions for a girl who grew up unprepared to fight for her life or others.

All secrets have a cost and Rouge-s determination to find the truth can only lead to trouble...or something even more sinister.

Free Books:

Did you love *Marked By Destiny*? Then you should read *Wash* by Lexy Timms and Sierra Rose!

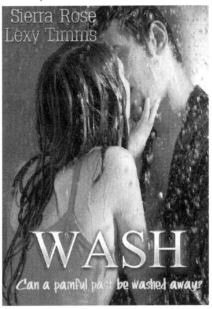

Can a painful past be washed away?2 Stories. 2 Loves. 2 Leading Ladies with Painful Pasts.Can love conquer all? Holding onto past pain and anguish is tortuous, it will never allow the emotion scarring to go away. Clinging to the past will never change your present. You have to let go so you can move forward with your life so you can hold your head up high. In Book 1, Ashly is haunted by her ex's actions when he dumped her at the altar. In Book 2, Charity has a rocky relationship with her father and tried to put the past behind her when she meets the sexy chief doctor at her father's hospital.

Also by W.J. May

Hidden Secrets Saga
Seventh Mark - Part 1
Seventh Mark - Part 2
Marked By Destiny

The Chronicles of Kerrigan
Rae of Hope
Dark Nebula
House of Cards

The Hidden Secrets Saga
Seventh Mark (part 1 & 2)

The Senseless Series
Radium Halos
Radium Halos - Part 2

Standalone
Shadow of Doubt (Part 1 & 2)
Five Shades of Fantasy

Glow - A Young Adult Fantasy Sampler
Shadow of Doubt - Part 1
Shadow of Doubt - Part 2
Four and a Half Shades of Fantasy
Full Moon
Marked By Destiny
Dream Fighter
What Creeps in the Night

Made in the USA
Middletown, DE
03 September 2015